The Crimson Tiger

The Crimson Tiger

short stories

DOUGLAS HARDING

The Shollond Trust
London

Published by The Shollond Trust
87B Cazenove Road, London N16 6BB, England
www.headless.org
headexchange@gn.apc.org

The Shollond Trust is a UK charitable trust, reg. no. 1059551

ISBN 978-1-908774-59-0

Many thanks to everyone who helped transcribe the stories.

Cover design by rangsgraphics.com
Interior design by Richard Lang

Contents

	Introduction	vii
1.	Mourning For Grandfather	3
2.	Esmeralda Brown	11
3.	The Flemish Giant	31
4.	Beetles	41
5.	The Bird Of Paradise	47
6.	The Stink	61
7.	The Plymouth Brother	71
8.	Gerald's Thunderbolt	79
9.	Miss Clarissa	85
10.	St. Sebastian	93
11.	The Peach	107
12.	Red Front!	117
13.	The Crimson Tiger	133
14.	The Nightmare Nose	145

Introduction

Douglas Harding (1909–2007) wrote what I think is the greatest work of philosophy of the 20th century: *The Hierarchy of Heaven and Earth*, published in 1952. At present this is a view shared by few people because *The Hierarchy* is barely known outside the small circle of those who appreciate Harding, and even fewer within that circle have actually read either the huge original book or the condensed version he wrote afterwards. (His better-known, more popular books are those he wrote from the 1960s onwards.) I understand that for many people my view will sound like the claim of a deluded disciple. Yet I am convinced that eventually history will recognise the extraordinary achievement, the hugely important breakthrough, of this *magnum opus*. Harding's view of the cosmos, its structure and functioning, described in *The Hierarchy* with great clarity and with astonishing breadth and depth, is a view that is not only true but also profoundly good and beautiful. It is a thrilling new departure in the way we see ourselves. Refreshingly modern, it is a science-based re-assessment of who and what we are that amounts to a major leap forward in human consciousness and understanding. It is, as its subtitle boldly declares, 'a new diagram of man in the universe'.

It is in this context that these stories are of special interest. If they had been written by someone else, then they would be no more than entertaining reflections on a childhood and youth lived in the early 20th century. But they gain in interest and significance because of who wrote them, for they provide an insight into the life and mind of a youngster who later became a great philosopher and spiritual teacher. These stories open an intimate window on Harding's early life—their autobiographical nature is only thinly disguised. In *Mourning for Grandfather* Harding introduces us to his paternal grandfather—what fun they had together! In *The Plymouth Brother* you meet his father whose steadfast faith in God, even under threat of death, profoundly inspired his son. In *The Peach* you witness his mother's anger. In *The Stink* you are present when it dawns on him that there's more to life than being liked... In *Beetles* you see how intensely curious he was about the world around him, and how sharply observant about the minutest details. In *Red Front!* you are caught up in Harding's youthful flirtation with communism.

There is also a good deal of honest self-reflection in these pages: in *The Flemish Giant* Harding shines a light on dark places in his young soul, and even more so in *The Nightmare Nose*. In this latter story he is disturbingly frank about the shame and disgust he felt about his nose — during adolescence it became the focus of his self-hatred. Few of us go so far, are so brave and candid, as to admit to such mortifying sentiments in public, or indeed are so psychologically self-aware and articulate. At one level Harding was inspired by a profound curiosity about himself and about life. He had a passionate desire to find out who he was. But it is easy to admit to such admirable feelings. Not so the darker forces that might also be at work. *The Nightmare Nose* leaves no doubt that the young Harding was from time to time in great pain. He was angry and bitter. Without him being aware at the time of where they were leading, these powerful feelings of unworthiness, self-loathing and alienation played havoc with his life. Wounded, he needed healing. Later, much later, Harding came to appreciate the value of this excruciating, morbid self-consciousness that too often reared its unwelcome head in his youth. He came to see it as a vital, irreplaceable piece of the puzzle that in the end helped steer, or rather drive, him to the truth and healing of who he really was. When at last he saw his True Self, the face he had hated at times so vehemently was ousted by, in a sense washed clean by, what Zen calls "one's bright and charming Original Face". A curse turned into a blessing. A blessing that Harding then passed on to many others.

Harding wrote these stories when he was 26 and 27 (1935–36). At this time he was also writing his first book, *The Meaning and Beauty of the Artificial*. This is a serious, well-researched, well-written, substantial work that explores the artificiality of the dividing line between our bodies and our tools. Harding pointed out that once you realise that you do not stop at your skin, once you have crossed over the apparent frontier between 'self' and 'not-self', then there are no further frontiers that you cannot also cross till in the end you find yourself including everything.

The many hours of solitary work, of sustained focus, that went into writing this first book and these stories are testament to the youthful Harding's self-discipline. And his ambition. As well as wanting to know who and what he was, the young Harding also dreamed of being a great man—a great writer and a great philosopher—and was determined to do everything in his power to achieve his goal.

Even so his focus on writing did not mean he neglected his professional work or shunned relationships. After graduating in architecture from University College in London in 1931, Harding worked in the City, after which he returned to Suffolk in 1933 to join a firm in Ipswich. The warmth and respect his architectural colleagues felt for him became apparent when he applied for, and got, a job in India managing a large team in a major architectural firm in Calcutta. In January 1937, shortly before he sailed for India with his pregnant wife, the secretary of The Suffolk Association of Architects was instructed "to write to you to say that your resignation was accepted with great regret", and that the members "wished put on record their appreciation of your services so freely given. They would very much miss your help in this work which had been of the greatest value." Harding had earned a reputation for being helpful and reliable. He was well-liked. These stories also show this attractive side of the young Harding, his generosity, his understanding and warmth, his compassion. And his humour. Read *Gerald's Thunderbolt* and you will laugh alongside Gerald as Gerald gets the last laugh...

A recurring theme in Harding's life and work was his amazement that there is anything at all. Why isn't there just nothing? How did existence, or the One, or Awareness, or whatever you want to call it—how did it launch itself into Being from the darkest night of non-being? Or, put differently, how did *you* come to be—you as who you really, really are? After this 'impossible' feat of Self-origination, of conjuring yourself out of nothing without help, of spontaneously appearing in this moment now!—what is not possible? Throughout all that happens abides this mystery, this miracle, this blessing—the fact that one is. That the One is. Harding the adult never tired of expressing his wonder at, his praise and gratitude for, the One's achievement of Being. But an embryonic awareness of this mystery was already alive in Harding the child. If you want to hear that consciousness stirring, described by the twenty-something-year-old Harding as he looks back into his childhood, then stand with the father of the man, the twelve-year-old Harding, by the graveside of his beloved grandfather and listen to his thoughts:

"At the graveside he had stood next Aunt Abigail and heard the parson read the Burial Service. He liked the words: "I am the resurrection, and the life… And whosoever liveth and believeth in me shall never die." He liked them partly because, as it happened, he had just read the same words in *The Tale of Two Cities*, and partly because they were so grand in themselves. As a matter of fact he liked nearly every text that began "I am …" No matter what it went on to say, or what the exact meaning was, Philip was impressed. Directly he began to wonder what the words meant, they seemed to be nonsense. But if he just listened to them they gave him a curious sensation. During the reading of the Burial Service he had been obliged to blink his eyes, to swallow repeatedly, and deliberately to contemplate the skull and cross-bones carved upon a nearby headstone."

Harding gathered his stories together and named the collection after one of them: *The Crimson Tiger*. This collection was not published in Harding's lifetime, though one of the stories, *Beetles*, was published in India in 1943. Apart from that, as far as I know none of the other stories have seen the light of day. So it is a delight to make them available now. After reading them, you will know and understand Douglas Harding in a new and more intimate way.

Richard Lang

stories

Chapter 1

Mourning For Grandfather

Never before in his life had Philip ridden in a horse cab, so he looked about with great interest. From where he was sitting, on the left side by the door and facing the horse, he had a view of his three aunts who were sitting bolt upright in a row on the opposite seat, and all that was going on outside the window.

The inside of the cab smelt of horse dung and mildew, mingled with eau-de-Cologne from Aunt Esther's handkerchief and brilliantine from cousin Joseph's hair. Though the window panes in both the doors had been lowered, the heat of the midday sun beating down on to the roof, and up from the torrid face of the road, made the cab as hot and as stuffy as an oven. The old nag in front ambled along at a snail's pace that created no draught at the windows. Philip held on to the brass handle of the door with the idea of cooling his hands, till his mother, who was sitting beside him, told him not to do so because it was dangerous. She told him that he would undoubtedly topple out of the coach and land on his nose in the road, if he continued to play with the handle. Instead, a wad of seat stuffing, that projected from a hole in the dog-eared upholstery, occupied his attention. Under cover of his knees, he began to pull out bits of flock and deposit them under the seat, while Aunt Esther turned a solemn and disapproving eye on him.

Like Philip she was dressed in black for the funeral. She wore a wide-brimmed black hat with a chequered band and a black veil, spangled at regular intervals with little black stars. Philip's gaze, penetrating the veil, discerned the taut contours of her face, her high cheek-bones, the stretched skin of her nose, the glisten of many beads of perspiration in the midst of her downy black moustache. Below the veil he could see a vein throbbing against the velvet band that encircled her neck, and the slightly soiled edge of her high collar, where its supporting bones rubbed the lace against her skin. Every now and then her left hand would hoist the veil, while her right dabbed at her eyes with a handkerchief screwed into a moist ball about the size of a walnut. Then the veil and the hands descended and all was as before.

The other aunts, Abigail and Naomi, closely resembled their sister, save for the fact that their handkerchiefs were less sodden and rose less frequently to their eyes.

Philip was far from weeping. He was uncomfortable, certainly. His Eton collar, which had been bought specially for the occasion, chafed his neck unbearably, and from time to time ascended several inches at the rear, for it had broken loose from its back-stud. He had to keep pressing it down and adjusting it so as to ease his neck. Since his fingers were clammy and none too clean, the collar was already covered with finger-prints. But in spite of his collar, his new black suit that was also vexatious, the heat, and the gloom of the cab and its occupants, he was not at all unhappy. Quite the contrary: he was very glad indeed to be away from school.

How jealous the boys had been when he told them that he was going to his grandfather's funeral! Some had not believed him and had plainly considered the funeral a fictitious one, a ruse. Others had talked about the possibility of their own grandparents' early death and had said that relations should never be so inconsiderate as to die during the holidays.

The dressing-up had been unpleasant. But the fifty-mile ride in the train with his mother had been extraordinarily diverting. Through the window he had seen a river full of ships with their white sails stretching half way to heaven, an owl asleep on the top of a post — for all the world like a spink (he meant sphinx) he informed his mother — and a hayrick on fire, with a lot of men pumping water onto it.

And he had enjoyed the funeral. The music in the church had put him in mind of old Happy Welham's barrel-organ, whose jingling tunes he loved; and the rumbling and mumbling of the bass had pleased him greatly. Giving vent to his appreciation, he had growled in his throat to imitate the organ, till his mother intervened. At the grave-side he had stood next Aunt Abigail and heard the parson read the Burial Service. He liked the words: "I am the resurrection, and the life … And whosoever liveth and believeth in me shall never die." He liked them partly because, as it happened, he had just read the same words in *The Tale of Two Cities*, and partly because they were so grand in themselves. As a matter of fact he liked nearly every text that began "I am …" No matter what it went on to say, or what the exact meaning was, Philip was impressed. Directly he began to wonder what the words meant, they seemed to be nonsense. But if he just listened to them they gave him a curious sensation. During the reading of the Burial Service he had been obliged to blink his eyes, to swallow repeatedly, and deliberately to contemplate the skull and cross-bones carved upon a nearby headstone.

A blowfly buzzed frantically at the window pane, with its nose glued to the glass. Philip, thinking that it would be happier outside along with other blowflies, put up his hand to catch it, but Aunt Esther, mutely reproachful, shook her head at him and busied herself with her handkerchief. Instead of catching the fly he rummaged at the hole in the seat again, and looked out of the window.

They were going through one of the town's main streets. Scarcely anyone was afoot on the dazzling white pavement. It was the kind of weather to make you lounge in cooler places, sip lemonade in the shadow of trees, or bathe in the river. Philip observed a stout lady with a face like a coal of fire, struggling along as though she might drop at any moment. The flowers on her parasol tattooed her features with their shadows in a very strange way, and the little dog she was leading jumped about as though the pavement scorched his paws. Then a shop, whose window was full of gleaming tools, came into view. It was the place where his grandfather had bought him a penknife.

A walk with grandfather had always been exciting. They would march along—grandfather huge, white-walrused, red-faced and happy, Philip minute, yellow-haired, chubby and happy too—pretending that they were soldiers on a campaign. Philip, who was always the commanding officer, would shout: "Quick March! Right Turn! Left Wheel! Form Fours!" in quick succession, and grandfather would meekly obey, in so far as it lay in his power. How the old fellow had laughed at the command "Form Fours!" and how they had argued about it!

Ah yes, he had been a nice old grandfather! It was a pity he was dead. But they had enjoyed themselves together. Philip smiled when he remembered how they had teased grandmother. Grandmother, a little old lady with a lace cap and swollen knuckles, would often say to Philip, "How doth the little busy bee," in order to remind him to do his lessons, and grandfather, with a sly look, would whisper in Philip's ear his own version of the next line:

"Behave so very like a flea."

Then grandmother would throw up her hands with a gesture of despair and scold the old man and the child good-naturedly, crying: "Six of one, half dozen of t'other" (whatever that might mean) and shoo them out into the garden as though they had been a couple of hens. Philip chuckled softy when he thought of his grandfather's face, winking at him as soon as her back was turned.

Aunt Esther coughed, shook her head, and frowned behind her veil. Philip at once looked serious again.

A heap of the flock stuffing now lay under the seat. He pulled out another tuft and dropped it on the floor, uncomfortably conscious of his aunt's moist eyes fastened upon him.

They had come to the barracks. Philip saw the sentry on duty at the gates, enduring the heat as steadfastly as if he had been the faithful-unto-death soldier in the picture, and at once recalled grandfather's oft repeated tale of the sentry at these same gates, who, one dark night, had shot off a donkey's tail because he couldn't answer the challenge: "Who goes there: friend or foe?"

They were always playing soldiers, he and his grandfather. Whenever Philip went to stay with his grandparents in the garrison town, there would be dressing-up and drill and martial events in the back garden. During his last visit they had been very thorough. Philip had felt that some visible evidence of his rank was needed — of course he was always a captain, or a drum major, or a field marshal, while grandfather was only a private, or on special occasions, as a reward for good behavior, a lance-corporal. Since there were six feet and more of grandfather and only about half that of Philip, however, the evidence had seemed to point all the other way. They had agreed that the situation, as it stood, was quite intolerable, and might lead to mutiny. Accordingly they had prepared a ferocious moustache from the beard of a cocoa-nut, bought a little — but not sufficiently little — scarlet coat and a peak cap from a fancy-dress shop, fashioned an entire armoury of swords and rifles out of lengths of wood, stolen the copper lid for a shield, cut down a pair of old trousers to suit the length of Philip's legs, and made an incomparable pair of spurs out of a couple of wish-bones, gilded and barbed with cog-wheels taken from an old alarum clock. All these accoutrements were gathered in utmost secrecy and stored in the garden shed. Grandmother had known by Philip's state of suppressed excitement that they were up to some mischief or other.

Then, one morning, when grandmother was busy picking weeds, she had been startled out of her wits by the blasting of a bugle on the other side of the hedge.

Up the garden path a pigmy warrior had come striding. His face was terrible with whiskers that left little showing but his eyes. A dazzling scarlet coat, trimmed with gold braid, reached to his calves; black trousers as voluminous as a couple of skirts, hung con-certina-fashion about his feet; a mighty shield stuck all over with devices in silver paper, weighed him down on one side; the other was bristling with swords, poniards and firearms. Grandfather, in his everyday black suit and winged collar, but with an enormous admiral's hat upon his head, brought up the rear. In his right hand he held a tin trumpet from which he produced ear-splitting noises. In his left he held a piece of string that was tied to the neck of the unwilling regimental mascot, Panther the cat, who had been decked with a paper crown and a yellow sash about her middle.

Grandmother had been quite speechless at the sight. Her hands had waved about irresolutely in the air, clutched at her apron and then gone up to her ears. Round and round the lawn the two soldiers had marched, under the apple trees and the pear trees, while Philip commanded and countermanded. Finally they had recruited grandmother, given her a big sword to brandish, and made her march behind the cat, upon pain of court-martial. Afterwards, Philip insisted eating his lunch with his whiskers intact, and the three of them spent most of the afternoon manoeuvring in the garden.

What a day! But the next evening they had gone to a concert in the town and listened to a negro choir singing spirituals. A song about Ezekiel's wheels had delighted Philip. But when the negroes began to sing

"I'll lay down my shield by the river-side
And study war no more,"

he exchanged glances with his grandfather and experienced a serious attack of gulping and blinking, such as had come over him half an hour ago, during the funeral service.

In the morning his grandfather had noticed the disappearance of the military accoutrements from the shed.

"Where are they gone?" he asked Philip.

"Down by the river-side."

"O yes... Yes of course."

They shook hands on it, firmly declaring that they would study war no more.

A day or two later grandfather had discovered him trying on the scarlet coat, which he had taken from its hiding-place by the ditch at the bottom of the garden. Philip went very red and tried to explain. But the difficulty was smoothed out very easily. Philip became a uniformed Red-Cross man, wounded his grandfather severely about the arms and legs, then swathed him in bandages and made him limp about the house, till grandmother intervened, declaring that he would become struck like that, and tempting Providence it was.

Philip laughed outright when he thought of it all. He checked himself at once, however, when he remembered where he was. But his three aunts were all looking at him reproachfully through their veils, and cousin Joseph — horrid lad — was leaning forward to see what had made him laugh. His mother, sitting stiffly by his side, gave him a powerful prod with her elbow.

Aunt Esther lifted her veil, mopped her eyes, then leaned towards him and said in a low, melancholy voice:

"Think of your grandfather, Philip."

"I was," Philip said timidly.

A pause, while Aunt Esther put her gloved hand on his knee and peered at him intently.

"You won't ever see him again, you know."

"I know."

"Never, never again in this world. Aren't you sorry?"

"Yes."

Everyone in the cab was looking at him. He felt their accusing eyes that seemed to rebuke him, saying:

"You don't love your grandfather. You aren't sorry. You laughed."

He closed his eyes. He knew that he ought be looking sad and crying now and then like his aunts. He tried to make himself weep a little by thinking about his grandfather's body lying in the coffin. But whenever he got the dead face clearly pictured in his mind, there was the absurd admiral's hat perched on top of it. He very nearly laughed again.

The cab jolted on. The creaking of the springs, the slow clicking of the horse's hoofs on the road and the buzzing of the bluebottle, furnished a monotonous accompaniment to his thoughts. The cab had reached the fringe of the town now. Still trees, hedgerows laden with white dust, and red cottages roasting in the sun, drifted by the window. He could feel his shirt sticking to him, his lips and tongue were dry, and muddy little rivers of sweat ran in the creases of his palms.

His thoughts wandered back to the funeral: "I am the resurrection and the life…" to Sidney Carton wandering in the streets of Paris, to the negroes and their song.

Aunt Esther and Philip were gazing fixedly at each other. She saw him shut his eyes and open them, blink repeatedly and stare in a queer manner. Then, suddenly, there were little convulsions in his throat, his small, freckled face wrinkled up, and a flood of tears poured down his cheeks.

She leaned forward with outstretched hands. He tumbled into her arms, shaking with sobs, clutching at her dress.

"There, there, dear," she said, stroking his hair tenderly.

His face was hidden against her dress. The three aunts exchanged glances and smiled.

"Dear boy. They were such friends," they whispered to one another…

Five minutes later Philip was back in his seat, with his eyes dried, pulling out the last shreds of stuffing.

A breeze, just strong enough to be perceptible, drifted in from the window. The gloom inside the cab seemed to have lifted. The women, whose tongues had been loosened, began to talk in hushed voices about the reading of the will, the journey home, the hot weather.

Philip was thinking how lucky it was that the funeral had occurred during the school term, instead of during the holidays. He grinned.

This time Aunt Esther smiled back at him.

* * *

Chapter 2

Esmeralda Brown

Esmeralda Brown is a small woman of thirty-five with fuzzy mouse-coloured hair and prominent teeth, who works during the day as a clerk in the Civil Service, and lives in a room in Lambs Conduit Street. Her dress is so startling that everyone stares at her. Every day she walks along High Holborn on the way to her office in a black cloak lined with green silk, and a sort of billycock hat which is green too and very high in the crown. Except in the severest weather she wears open-work sandals. During Guy Fawkes' Month (it is a month in these parts) the urchins sometimes walk beside her with their caps held out for coppers, shouting "Penny for the guy, mister!" Though she has been wearing clothes like these for some time, she doesn't appear to be quite comfortable in them. You get the feeling that she is aware of them all the time.

Her room in Lambs Conduit Street is at the top of a long flight of stairs, over a pork butcher's shop. It is a smallish low room with a sloping ceiling and a dormer window that commands a view of a parapet wall some three feet away. Between the window and the parapet there is a lead gutter where Esmeralda sun-bathes whenever it is warm enough. Ever since she started reading D. H. Lawrence, she has prostrated herself during week-ends in the gutter, alternately exposing her front and her back to the sun. Lying there she cannot be seen, but getting in and out of the window in her dressing gown, taking it off while lying flat, and even turning over, are difficult things to do without exposing herself to curious eyes. She has also to keep a watch for men mending telegraph wires and roofs, and the folk in the attic opposite—but Esmeralda will not be deterred.

Inside the room there are a lot of books, of which she is very proud. They are surprisingly various. Well-thumbed works on astrology and palmistry are ranged alongside the Santayana and the Croce that she has never read a page of, though she often mentions them, making Croce rhyme with dose. Thomas A'Kempis rubs covers with yellow backed Paul de Cock; Stephen Spender is next to Ella Wheeler Wilcox; *Poise, Personality and Power*, by Homer Q. Twine jostles *War and Peace*; and there are rows of books about the way to make life happy and glorious by living on nut and herbs, or thinking Right Thoughts, or avoiding constipation, or being a Love Radiation, or masticating every mouthful thirty times, or sleeping, waking, speaking, remaining silent, doing nothing, doing everything, in some peculiar way, every one of which Esmeralda has tried.

She has a passion for gimcracks, curious gadgets for which she is always searching the windows of second-hand shops. Miniature birds and beasts—lambs and pigs and ostriches and donkeys, made of china and wood and brass—adorn the mantelpiece, the window ledge, and the tops of the bookcases. She has little dogs with legs formed of pipe-cleaners, a set of minute porcelain giraffes and wildebeest, and a chromium plated elephant. There is a cockatoo with a saucy crimson face, and a naughty statuette bought in Paris. And there are barley-sugar candles which she calls 'dinky', and a bowl of incense that she burns to give the room a voluptuous smell.

The pictures resemble the books in number and variety. They crowd the walls so that there is scarcely a foot of plaster showing. There are prints of Gauguin and Alma-Tadema, of Picasso and Poynter, of Matisse and Wyllie; but above all, occupying the points of vantage, are originals by the English painter Frekk. Over the fireplace hangs a large oil-colour of his in a silvered frame, an abstract composition of geometrical figures and writhing lines that look like serpents. On the opposite wall is a smaller work of Frekk's, a nude of Esmeralda herself, and on top of the piano is a pen-and-ink portrait of Frekk, who appears as a young man with a hooked nose and a long face.

If you get into conversation with Esmeralda Brown, she will tell you, in the first ten minutes, that she was to have married Frekk, the brilliant young painter, who died a year ago, and she will let drop a hint that she had been his mistress. She will tell you of his picture in the Tate, of his untimely death, of their love for one another. And you will be surprised at such an alliance. Everyone is.

This is what actually happened:

Six months after Esmeralda Brown took the attic in Lambs Conduit Street, Frekk the painter moved into the room beneath, on the second floor.

At that time Esmeralda had not acquired the habit of wearing a cloak or a billycock hat, nor had she bought her prints of Modern Masters. Her books were almost entirely devoted to the culture of the Soul, the Personality, and the Body Beautiful. She brewed and drank gallons of a liquid, made of some herb or other, which she called 'coffee'; she subsisted on grated carrots, chopped dates, and lettuce leaves, and she prostrated herself at regular intervals in the gutter.

It was the coming of Frekk which made the difference. Sometimes she met him on the stairs when she was returning from the office, and in the bathroom-scullery which all the tenants in the house shared. He was a tall, loose-limbed fellow with a face as long as a horse's, very big dark eyes and thick lips. He looked as though he hadn't been to sleep for weeks — an attractively dissipated appearance some people said it was, but Esmeralda called it aesthetic, spiritual. His hair was long and iron grey, and he wore a loose fitting Norfolk jacket that was ancient and daubed with paint. He used to peel his potatoes over the sink in the bathroom, and Esmeralda, while holding her lettuce under the tap, would try to get into conversation with him, asking him what he painted, how he cooked the potatoes, and so forth. But all the answer he gave was a look at her with his big eyes and a grunt.

Models used to come and sit for Frekk, and Esmeralda thought some of them were very beautiful. When the door bell rang, each of the front tenants used to look out of the windows to see who the caller was, in order to save coming downstairs on some other tenant's behalf. Esmeralda was constantly looking out and seeing one of Frekk's women on the doorstep. He didn't stick to one model;

there were at least four who came regularly and Esmeralda got to know them all by sight. She would hear Frekk's boots go plonk plonk down the stairs as he went to let them in. There would come laughter and talking, then a long silence, and sometimes she heard peculiar sounds, the floor was so thin. Esmeralda was intrigued.

One day she asked him if she might peel his potatoes for him. He was quite willing. The next day she helped him again and discovered that he had nothing to go with them. She ran up to her room and prepared a big dish of salad and brought it down to his room. Again, he was quite willing to take it and Esmeralda was delighted. She sat on a cushion in his studio watching him while he ate in silence, shovelling in great mouthfuls of food as though he could go on forever.

His room, or studio, was bigger than Esmeralda's, and nearly empty. The boards were bare and the only furniture consisted of a wooden chair, a deal table, a bed, some cushions and, of course, his painter's paraphernalia. He was obviously very poor. She fetched him some fruit and nuts, and he ate those up too. He must have been famished, she thought.

After he had done eating she asked to see some of his paintings. He showed them to her. Most of them were very modern, but there were a few portraits in the more conventional manner. Esmeralda clasped her hands, stood in an attitude of rapt admiration, and tried to think of a suitable word. 'Charming' was the only expression that came into her head, so she said it. Frekk appeared to be quite annoyed. However, after they had looked at all the paintings, he mumbled some sort of thanks for the food and she went up to her room again, as he plainly wanted to work.

Nearly every evening after that she took something down to his room, or left it for him by the door if he had a model there. He never said much, but once he hinted that he wasn't very fond of 'rabbits' food', so she bought steaks and rashers of bacon and pork chops for him and cooked them on her gas stove, and now and then she got him a bottle of beer. All her health principles—vegetarianism, teetotalism, non-smoking, even sunbathing—went by the board. At the office she surprised everyone by the sudden change in her. She grew off-hand with her old friends, scarcely opening her mouth except to say something high-falutin about Art, or something disparaging about the office and the people in it. And she began, casually, to mention her friend the painter.

But the models came to see Frekk regularly, and Esmeralda would listen intently to hear what was going on underneath. At meal-times she would sometimes take two plates of food down to his room, one for him and the other for his friend. On these occasions she ate alone, upstairs. Once, having knocked at his door, she thought she heard him say "Come in," and in she went. She saw the model's clothes on the floor and his lying beside them, and hurriedly backed out again. Such happenings made Esmeralda sulk a little in private, but she went on supplying Frekk with meals as before.

During the cold weather she discovered that he was working without a fire, so she lent him her oil stove and replenished it with paraffin whenever necessary. When she went in his room to attend to it he would look at her in a curious sort of way, with an amused gleam in his eyes and an inscrutable expression. He rarely said more than a word or two. She didn't mind his silence. In fact, she admired it tremendously.

"He has the artistic temperament," she would say to her friends. "He lives for his Art."

Whatever else Frekk did or omitted to do, he certainly did work. He worked all day and every day as long as the light lasted, and the pile of canvases in the corner of his room grew bigger and bigger. Every now and then he went to the Caledonian Market and picked up a number of old oil-colours almost for nothing, which he used to paint over, instead of buying new canvases. One day, in response to a question, he told Esmeralda that he was working for a one-man exhibition. She was delighted and wanted to know whether she could help in some way. Wouldn't he prefer new canvases, for instance? No, he didn't want any new canvases, but Esmeralda bought him tubes of the more expensive colours, which he couldn't afford. It gave her a great deal of pleasure to help him in this way. She felt she was doing something for Art.

Esmeralda's sudden interest in Art took her to the Tate, The National Gallery and Burlington House. She bought books about painting, some of which she read. From these she learned a few impressive words like *chiaroscuro* and Fauviste and Post-Impressionism, which she trotted out whenever the occasion seemed to warrant their use. She tried very hard, too, to discover which paintings she ought to admire, and in what terms she should express her admiration. Frekk was not at all useful in such matters: when she timidly asked his opinion of Brangwyn he just looked at her, emitted a sort of throaty chuckle, and said, "Good God!" with that amused look in his eyes. Hitherto she had admired paintings that were like photographs for verisimilitude, and those which, like pictures of dogs and horses and lovers, excited her sympathies. It now appeared that she had been on altogether the wrong tack. It didn't matter—so the book said, and so Frekk's paintings seem to say—whether a painting of a horse looked more like a rolling-pin than a horse, so long as it gave you a mysterious feeling. As for subject—a composition might be anything, all lines and spots, or nothing more than an inverted pyramid, and still be reckoned a masterpiece!

So Esmeralda took down the pictures in her room which she felt did not conform to her new standards, and stacked them in the cupboard. In their places she put prints of moderns, whose names she had learned from her book. She was very proud of her new pictures, and if any of her acquaintances dared to breathe a word of dislike of them, or of regret for the old ones, she did not hesitate to use the word 'philistine.' Whenever, in her tours of the galleries, she came upon an abstract painting or anything at all curious, she would stand and look at it for a long while, memorizing every detail. Then she would tell people how wonderful it was. 'Wonderful', she found, was a safe and useful word. From time to time she divulged scraps of her new knowledge to Frekk, who just stared and said nothing.

One day she saw a handsome Spanish looking woman at one of the galleries, talking to a man about the pictures. Esmeralda overheard what they were saying. They were connoisseurs, obviously; the genuine thing. And the lady looked wonderfully artistic and interesting in her cloak. Esmeralda appeared, a week later, in one almost exactly like it. Without exception her office acquaintances were nasty about the new cloak, but that only served to confirm what she had known all along: they were 'rank outsiders', quite hopeless.

Not even her new clothes appeared to have any effect on Frekk. This had begun to depress her, when suddenly their relations took a new turn.

Esmeralda was sitting alone in her room one evening, thinking about him and wondering what next she could do to interest him, when Frekk himself knocked at her door and walked in. It was the first time he had ever gone into her room; she had never been able to persuade him to come up. Esmeralda's face was radiant. She asked him to sit down in the easy chair by the fire and proffered a cigarette. She sat on a cushion at his feet, looking up at his face.

He looked haggard today, very dark and baggy about the eyes, which were so big and bright that Esmeralda began to think that he had something of great importance to tell her, something personal and moving. His long grey hair looked peculiarly crinkled and dry. She noticed, when he put out his enormous hand to take the cigarette, that it shook more than usual.

"You've been working too hard," she said, smiling up at him.

He chuckled down in his throat in his usual fashion.

Esmeralda shifted just a shade nearer. For once he did not draw back.

"Do you like my Picasso?" she asked, pointing to one of the pictures.

"Well…" he said, then blew out a stream of smoke and regarded it solemnly.

"I think it's wonderful. What splendid massing, and grouping of elements!"

At that he looked surprised, and whistled.

After a while she asked him when his exhibition was going to be held.

"Christ knows," he said.

"It will be marvellous, wonderful!"

"Hm."

Then they were silent again, and she moved a little nearer.

Quite suddenly, he said, "The landlord's going to chuck me out. Arrears."

She leaned her head on his knee.

"How much do you want?"

He appeared to think for a moment, then said, "Twenty Pounds."

Esmeralda got up and found her cheque book. She had saved a little money during her seventeen years at the Post Office, so she made out a bearer cheque for twenty five pounds and gave it to him with a smile.

He smiled too, when he took it, for the first time during their acquaintance. She nestled up against his knees, and presently felt his hand touching her hair.

"I'll pay you back sometime," he said.

"No, it's yours." She nestled closer. "On one condition."

He chuckled. "Well?"

"That you paint me."

She gave a little cry of delight when he consented.

He got up and went back to his work.

The next day, being a half holiday, Esmeralda went shopping in Shaftesbury Avenue. At an establishment that went in for smart, seductive underwear, she bought a lot of garments that were diaphanous and trimmed with lace and ribbons, a pair of very high-heeled shoes and two pairs of black silk stockings. And she called at a shop that was covered with big notices about pills for weak men and female irregularities, and whose window was full of artificial limbs.

When she got back to Lambs Conduit Street she encountered Miss Solent on the staircase. Miss Solent was the lady who lived on the first floor.

"Have you heard the news?" she asked Esmeralda.

"What news?"

"That Frekk is throwing a bottle party tonight. I'm going. Are you?"

"Why yes," replied Esmeralda, who had not heard of the party. She loathed Miss Solent.

Esmeralda waited a long time for Frekk to come up and invite her to the party, but he didn't come. She took a pot of tea down for him. He was not alone, so she set the tray down outside the door and went upstairs again to dress for the party. She performed her toilet with great care and put on her party dress and ruby ear-rings. Then the guests started coming. She crept out into the gutter and looked down at them, taking care not to be seen. They arrived in twos and threes. She recognized some of the women, and there were men who looked as though they might be artists, fellows with beards and long hair, holding bottles in their hands and making so much noise that they appeared to be tipsy already.

Esmeralda began to feel excited and nervous at the prospect of meeting such remarkable people. She wondered what they would talk about — painting, perhaps — and she rehearsed a few things to say. And she wondered how she would look in her party dress, whether they would like her, whether the women were as beautiful as they looked in the distance, whether she would be very embarrassed.

Underneath, in Frekk's room, there was a great hubbub, sounds of laughter and vivacious talking and the chinking of glasses. Esmeralda climbed back again into her room and waited. Two hours later she was still waiting.

The noise below had been increasing steadily, the conversation becoming more animated, the songs — which she could hear perfectly — more boisterous and bawdy, and the laughter that followed the stories — she presumed they were stories — more hilarious. Apparently one of the guests had brought a concertina, to whose strains they began to dance with much stamping, so that the whole building shook. Esmeralda lay on her bed listening and waiting.

After the dancing, the party became much quieter; the concertina played fitfully, then drunkenly, then not at all. Presently the door of the room below opened and someone began to climb the stairs. It was him—Frekk—she knew his heavy tread at once. At last, at last he was coming up to ask her to the party!

But the footsteps halted half way up the staircase that led to her room. Perhaps he was drunk. She would go to him! Opening the door, she looked down. The stairs were quite dark and she could see nothing at all, but there came sounds—a woman's giggle and then that chuckle of Frekk's and a shuffling. She shut the door again, undressed and went to bed, but not until dawn did she fall asleep.

The next day and the day after, Esmeralda left tea and food outside his room, but, though he was alone, she did not knock at the door. She passed him once on the stairs and said nothing, looking straight ahead. She met him again at the sink, and this time he looked at her and said,

"What's the matter?"

She stared at him and bit her lip.

"What's the matter?" he repeated.

She turned and went upstairs without replying.

Frekk asked Miss Solent's opinion as to the reason for Miss Brown's conduct. She told him what Esmeralda had said to her on the staircase, about the party.

The next time she left something outside his door, he appeared and asked her to come in.

Awkwardly, in that explosive, gruff way of his, he apologized.

"I didn't know… I… had no idea you wanted to come to that party. "

Esmeralda asked if she might get her lunch and have it with him.

"Why yes, do," he said.

Presently they were both at the table eating away, she seated on the bed, he on the one chair.

"Thought somehow you wouldn't like them. Not quite your sort," he resumed.

Esmeralda's face puckered up at that, as though he had hit her.

"What… what do you mean, not my sort?" she said, controlling her voice.

"Well… er…" he hunted for a word.

"I'm not a prude."

"No, of course not."

"Well what is it then?"

"O nothing, I suppose. Just an idea. I'm sorry, though, very sorry."

Esmeralda smiled. "Let's forget about it," she said, and they continued to eat in silence.

"When are you going to paint me?" she asked, after they had finished.

"I'll start right away, if you like."

"This afternoon?"

"Yes."

Esmeralda tried in vain to conceal her gratitude and pleasure. She cleared the table and took the dirty dishes to the sink, then went up to her room and got ready. Presently she came down again with a dressing gown slung over her arm, carrying a lighted oil stove.

He was still sitting in the chair, smoking his pipe. His fat red lips projected half way up the pipe stem and the pipe shook, as though he were laughing inwardly.

"A nude, hey?"

"Don't you want it to be?"

"Ah ah."

He got up and looked for a suitable canvas and started rigging it up on the easel. Then he occupied himself squeezing out colours on to his palette.

Meanwhile Esmeralda was undressing. She took off her dress and her petticoat, and stood waiting. She was wearing the underclothes that she had bought in Shaftesbury Avenue, and her high-heeled shoes and black silk stockings. She stood there, looking at the floor and blushing violently, waiting to hear what he would say. She did not know that his back was turned.

"Ready?" he asked, without turning round.

Esmeralda waited. Still he did not turn round. She finished

undressing and sat down on some cushions. She had a squat little body with big hips and waist, and very narrow shoulders; and her skin was dotted here and there, between her breasts and on her shoulders, with little pink spots. She let her hair down. It hung in a mouse coloured mop nearly down to her waist. Her breasts were thin and purse shaped and flopped down on her stomach.

"How would you like me to pose?" she said, smiling.

He turned round and stared at her. His pipe wobbled in his mouth, but his face was inscrutable.

"Lie out a bit more. Rest your head on your hand and get comfortable."

She did so, while he surveyed her critically. Then he fetched the cover from the bed and suspended it from the mantelpiece to form a background. Having shifted the easel, he looked at her again, frowning.

"Relax. Don't lie so awkwardly," he said.

"Come and show me how you mean."

"O you're alright, I guess," he answered, with a chuckle.

He sketched in the main lines.

"Do you want me to smile?" said Esmeralda, showing all her teeth.

"What?" said Frekk, "Good God, no." He went on sketching.

After fifteen minutes, Esmeralda felt desperately uncomfortable. Her arm was going dead, her hip was inadequately cushioned, and there came a chilly draught from under the door. But she didn't want to interrupt him. At the end of half an hour, she was really in pain.

"Want a rest?" he asked her.

She got up and ran on tiptoe to look at the canvas, her breasts flapping against her body.

"How clever!" she cried, standing beside him. He sniffed and relit his pipe while she laid her hand on his arm.

"It must be wonderful to paint like that," she said.

Frekk squeezed out some more colour on to his palette. After ten minutes' rest they started off again. Then the doorbell rang.

Frekk opened the window and looked out.

"It's someone for me," he said, shutting the window again.

"Oh, dear! Shall I go?"

"Stay right where you are."

He went down to let his visitor in. It was a woman. Esmeralda could hear him chatting on the stairs.

Presently they came in. Esmeralda recognized the woman at once as one of his models. Frekk introduced them with a wave of his hand:

"Judith — Miss Brown."

Esmeralda's face went pink and she gave a sickly but broad smile, while Judith sat on the bed, saying,

"Don't let me stop you." Her manner was completely self-possessed, her voice smooth.

Frekk went on painting while Esmeralda and the girl inspected each other.

To Esmeralda she looked terribly handsome, and terribly sure of herself. She was big and plump, and dressed up to make the most of her bouncing figure. A white beret, worn very much to one side, showed off her lustrous jet-black hair. Her face was serenely provocative, her bosom, so far as one could tell, of classical roundness and proportions. She stared at Esmeralda's prostrate form, with a sort of half-smile on her lips.

Judith smoked a cigarette while Frekk worked. Then she looked at the painting, coughed, and announced her intention to go. Frekk showed her to the front door. Esmeralda overheard Frekk's chuckle as they parted.

"Who was that?" she asked when he returned.

"Oh, a model."

"She's very beautiful."

"Ah."

"Have you known her long?"

"Ah," Frekk sounded preoccupied with his painting.

All the afternoon she sat for him, till it was dusk. After he had cleaned his brushes and put his colours away she still lay there, on the floor.

"Well," he said at length, "That's all for today."

She walked over and lay down on the bed.

"I'm so tired," she said, sighing.

He filled his pipe and lit it, taking no notice of her.

"What about a cup of tea?" she said.

"No thanks, I'm going out." He put on his overcoat.

On the following Saturday and Sunday Esmeralda sat again, and the picture neared completion. But the week-end after, Esmeralda was obliged to spend in the country, with Alice her elder sister.

She told Alice about Frekk, what a gifted painter he was, how attractive he looked, of the portrait. Esmeralda was in high spirits and secretly felt sorry for her sister, a simple countrified soul who knew nothing about Art, or artistic people. Alice was a district nurse and kindness itself, and she admired Esmeralda tremendously.

"Of course, you've always been the bright one of the family. Clever and interesting. I'm afraid I should feel quite lost among your brilliant friends," Alice said lovingly.

"Poor Alice," thought Esmeralda.

When she arrived at the house in Lambs Conduit Street on Monday evening, the first thing that she noticed was that the curtains of Frekk's room had gone. She knocked at his door and there came no answer. All the evening not a sound rose from his room. She lay in bed listening for him to come in, but he never came.

In the morning she called on Miss Solent and asked her if she knew what had befallen Frekk.

"Didn't you know?" said Miss Solent in her iciest tone. "He cleared out on Saturday. Hopped it, wheeling all his gear away on a hand-cart."

"Where did he go?" Esmeralda was trying to appear calm.

"I haven't the faintest idea. Why, did he owe you something?"

"Oh no, nothing. Only—he lent me a book and I wanted to return it," Esmeralda lied breathlessly.

"Didn't know he had any books," said Miss Solent, in her contemptuous way.

Esmeralda waited to hear from him, examining the letters eagerly every morning and evening. She went to see the landlord but he knew nothing. She inserted notices in the personal columns of newspapers. It was no good. Frekk had vanished from Lambs Conduit Street without leaving a clue as to his destination. Esmeralda's face developed a worn look.

After all her efforts to trace him had failed, she remembered that he had been in the habit of going to one of the Bloomsbury taverns in the evening—to which one she did not know. Very likely it was to the Sun & Stars, just off Tottenham Court Road. So Esmeralda went there, evening after evening, to find him.

She would go in very timidly, order a gin-and-it, and retire with it to a corner, where she sat in a state of utter misery gazing at the people who came in. She got to know their faces by sight—the dirty-looking old woman, often very tipsy, who resembled a charwoman but was really a poet, the youth called Davie, with his fantastic curls and make-up, who invariably carried a Pekinese under his arm, the cross-eyed girl who would lean over the bar counter all the evening without speaking to anyone till closing time, when she usually went off with one of the men, and other more or less peculiar folk—artists, or models, or students.

On Saturday and Sunday nights the company was always larger and more lively. The mechanical piano, next to which Esmeralda used to sit, played deafeningly almost all the time, and everyone talked and laughed at once except the cross-eyed girl and Esmeralda. Sometimes there would be a quarrel and a fight or someone would get roaring drunk, and then a barman would come and throw the offender out. On one occasion a girl mounted a chair, hitched up her skirt several inches, and conducted a mock auction of her favours for the night. Esmeralda sat in her corner drinking gin-and-its, trying to get into a fit condition to enjoy her surroundings. But the more she drank the more out of place and wretched she felt and looked.

Nevertheless at the office next morning she did not fail to mention to the girl who worked with her that she had spent the previous evening in the company of artists, and in her letters to her sister she wrote about her 'Bohemian friends'.

After two months, during which she drank a sufficient quantity of gin-and-it to undo the effect of all of the health exercises that she had ever performed, she found, not Frekk, but the model Judith, sitting alone in the *Sun & Stars* early one evening. Esmeralda—she was wearing her cloak and a species of sombrero—went and sat down beside Judith, and blurted out,

"Where's Frekk?"

Judith stared.

"You remember, he was painting me when you called one afternoon." Esmeralda added. "Where is he?"

Judith looked her up and down, observing everything. Esmeralda's appearance had not improved. Her little speckled face was thinner and it peered out from under the hat like the face of some stricken, old-looking waif. Her cloak formed a black pyramid, so that she seemed to have no shoulders at all, and the enormous hat looked like a sort of finial.

"I would never have recognized you," said Judith still staring.

"*Where's* Frekk?" Esmeralda insisted.

"Now what do you want him for?"

"O, he has something of mine," replied Esmeralda, off-handedly.

"Over Sabatelli's in Percy Street, on the top floor. I guess he'll be pleased to see you."

Esmeralda ran off immediately to Percy Street. She rang the doorbell next to Sabatelli's. A frowsy woman appeared and demanded in an angry voice, "Well?"

"Is Mr. Frekk here?"

"Yes he is"

"May I see him?"

"Yes, I reckon so."

"And you can tell him from me that I an't goin' to wait another day for all the rent he owes me," the woman added as they went upstairs.

Esmeralda knocked at the door, heard his voice say "Come in," and entered.

He lay in bed. At once she saw that his face was quite white and his beard inches long, making his features look even more elongated and ghastly. His eyes were appallingly large and diffused with blood. He was ill, very ill.

Esmeralda ran up to the bed, and stood over him. He turned his head slowly and looked at her, chuckling deep down in his throat almost in his old way.

"Oh it's you," was all he said.

Esmeralda plied him with questions—how ill was he, had a doctor been to see him, why hadn't he let her know, and why, O why had he left her, without a word or a note?

He sighed wearily and stared at her, grimacing slightly.

She looked round the room. It was small and ill lit. There were his old things—the bed, the chair, the table, that he had shifted from Lambs Conduit Street on the handcart, and his easel and canvases were stacked in a corner. The landlady had supplied a washstand and a chest of drawers.

"You owe some rent?" she asked him.

"Yes."

She went out and discovered the landlady waiting on the landing. The woman explained:

Frekk had been ill for a month. The doctor had called several times, but he had not said what the trouble was. She gathered it was serious enough. Did many people come to see him? No. At first they did. But after she told them about the arrears of rent they stopped coming. She couldn't run her establishment on charity, that she couldn't, and the waiting on him hand and foot was something cruel.

Esmeralda asked how much he owed.

"Not far off a fiver," replied the woman.

Esmeralda promised to let her have the money and to come and look after him at night.

"If you ask me, he's going to snuff it," the woman whispered in Esmeralda's ear.

For the next two months Esmeralda nursed him every night, while she continued to work during the day at her office. Lord knows how she did it. But she was happy, oh yes she was happy. He depended on her entirely. She paid the rent and the doctor's bills; prepared his food, gave him his medicine, washed him, performed the most intimate duties, attended to everything. Art and everything else vanished from her letters and conversation. Even her cloak was temporarily cast off.

Frekk remained mild and silent. He was growing weaker daily. Daily she felt that he was more and more hers.

One afternoon, while Esmeralda was at work, Judith, the model, went to see him. He was quite conscious.

"Do you know what this Miss Brown has been saying?" she asked him.

"No—what?"

"That you and she were"—she hesitated, correcting herself—"are going to get married."

"Oh my God," he groaned, "For Christ's sake don't let her in here again. Oh my God..."

"Who will look after you?"

His bleached face wrinkled as though he were trying to muster his thoughts.

"Look here," he said earnestly, holding the girl's arm, "Swear to me that you will tell everyone what I think of her. Everyone, you understand. Advertise it... And if anything happens to me, tell her."

He gripped the girl's arm till it hurt. She promised.

Two days later, when Esmeralda arrived at Percy Street, she found him dead.

He was hers completely now. She wept, but her tears were tears of triumph as much as defeat; they were luxurious tears—tears of consummation. He was her own now, entirely, irrevocably.

That night she spent in his room, alone with him. It was the first night she had spent alone with him. In her fancy it was a kind of wedding night.

That is what actually happened.

Esmeralda Brown now wears a signet ring of Frekk's — the ring that he used to wear on his little finger. She tells people that he gave it to her a week before he died, as their engagement ring.

Judith has nothing to say.

* * *

Chapter 3

The Flemish Giant

The Flemish Giant wore a long silky coat of steel-blue hair. Flapping against its shoulders as it hopped about hung its lanky, tender ears, and their insides were purplish and smooth like the petals of some monstrous, fleshy orchid. It was a bulky, big-boned animal, with a fine pair of haunches, but in spite of its name and its size it was as meek as a mouse. Its round, deep-brown eyes beamed upon the world with an expression of serenity and mildness; its little grey nose was always working up and down, always active and a-sniff, humbly beseeching for things good to eat.

Paul, a wiry, unsmiling boy of thirteen with a shock of black hair tumbling about his forehead, was enthusiastic about the Flemish Giant. He had taken a fancy to the rabbit the moment he caught sight of it in the naturalist's shop window. It was bigger and sleeker than all the Dutch rabbits and Belgian hares and Angoras that the man in the shop could show him, and it cost no more than two and six. Paul had brought the Flemish Giant home in a wicker basket, and would have let it share his bed for the night, had not the maid threatened to complain to his mother.

In the morning Paul got up before breakfast, found a large packing-case in the cellar, and began to make it into a hutch. He contrived a door out of an old picture-frame that happened to be of the right size, filling half of it with wire netting and the other half with plywood. Before lunch he carried the hutch down to the bottom of the garden, on his back. In a secret place, behind a great barrier of artichoke plants that were taller than himself, he reared a pedestal of old bricks and set the hutch on top of it. A sheet of corrugated iron that lay nearby made an excellent roof. Sawdust and wisps of hay gave the hutch a snug look, and a pudding-basin full of water completed the furnishings. The Flemish Giant was put into its new quarters. It seemed to like them.

Paul spent all the afternoon at the bottom of the garden. Every ten minutes or so he would take the rabbit out of its hutch, nurse it on his lap, stroking its fur and offering it all kinds of leaves or a little rice pudding stolen from the larder, and admire everything from the tip of its sensitive nose to its queer, fluffy tail. Then he let it hop about on the ground till it became lost among the artichoke stems, and was only caught after a long chase.

At length, tiring of this kind of play, Paul cycled into the town, bought packets of oats and bran, and gathered handfuls of greenstuff from the hedgerows on the way back. The Flemish Giant almost disappeared from view in the midst of all this provender. In the evening Paul cleared the hutch, gave it a thorough cleaning-out, and put down a new floor of sawdust and hay. Then, as a protection against draughts and the chilly night air, he draped an old overcoat about the hutch, bade the rabbit good-night, and retired early to bed on purpose to make plans for the animal's future.

The first thing was to give it a name. After reviewing all the historical names he could remember, Paul decided that Pepin was the most peculiar and therefore the most suitable of them all. This name, then, should be painted upon the lintel, and the whole exterior of the hutch should be painted white and red to accord with the dignity of its tenant. Proper hinges, instead of the wire loops that Paul, in his hurry, had been obliged to provide, were also necessary. A felt roof, too, would look better than the sheet of corrugated iron. There were, in fact, a score of things to do.

Next day Paul exhausted his entire savings on paint and roofing felt and hinges for the hutch and worked hard all day hammering, painting and screwing, while the Flemish Giant hopped about in a temporary pen with sides built of bricks, which Paul had set up on the grass near the hutch. By dusk, the hutch was a splendid sight. The sides were glossy white with scarlet edgings and scarlet letters along the lintel, and the roof was well tilted to throw off the rain and covered with black felt, that had a coating of grey dust upon it, like the bloom on a grape. Paul was sure, by the way the Flemish Giant frisked round and round sniffing at everything, that it was delighted with its new home.

When, two days later, the paint was nearly dry, Paul applied a second coat and picked out the edges and lettering more neatly. But this, and the combing of the rabbit's coat, and the provision of fresh food and water, and the daily cleansings of the hutch, left him with plenty of time to spare. He tried, without any success, to teach the Flemish Giant some simple tricks, and presented it with every kind of herbage imaginable. And, at intervals, he read all that he could find about wild and domesticated rabbits.

Still there was not enough to keep him busy, and Paul became restive. He had to find something else to do. Before the coming of the Flemish Giant, a telephone communicating with the next house had held his attention. First it had merely been a pair of cocoa tins connected by a length of string, a device which Paul and his friend next door had contrived jointly, in order to talk to each other at night. Then a second-hand field telephone had taken its place, and every night for a week the boys had talked until the early hours of the morning. Then Paul's friend had gone to the seaside for a holiday; he was there still, alas. The only person left for Paul to call up was the maid, and she was neither entertaining to talk to nor a willing listener. The telephone, formerly a mine of interest, was now quite worked out.

Before the phase of the telephone, Paul had spent most of his time practising archery in the garden, with his long-bow made of ground-ash and his arrows barbed with heads cut out of salmon tins. For a week or two it had proved an absorbing sport. And in the early months of the year he had lived for nothing but football. So it had been since he was a very small boy — one thing or another interested him to the exclusion of all else. For the time being he worked at, and thought about, and dreamed of that thing alone.

And ever since his early childhood there had been gaps, periods of transition from one enthusiasm to another, when he became irritable and morose, not knowing what to do with himself. Such a period had now come. The Flemish Giant had begun to bore him to distraction.

One afternoon, however, there came a diversion. Paul was invited to the house of a lady called Mrs. Pimgrove, who had a seventeen year old son named Oscar. Mrs. Pimgrove, a corpulent lady whose ankles were as fat as her calves, wore a hat that resembled a peach melba; and her son, whom Paul admired rather than liked, was scraggy and pimpled and looked as though he thought a great deal. They had tea on the lawn and talked about the flies, the curious taste of bread and butter eaten in the open air, and the cooling effect of tea on a hot day. While Mrs. Pimgrove mopped her brow with a table napkin, Paul attempted to bisect wasps with a knife, and Oscar, in a fine, gloomy manner, sought in vain to improve the quality of the conversation. He soon gave up the task and relapsed into a profound silence.

After tea, Oscar led Paul to a room that was lined with book-shelves and had a mahogany desk in the middle, on which lay a microscope, a reading-lamp, and heaps of papers. Paul sat down in the swivel chair while Oscar, in stately language, explained that the room was his private study, that the papers bore reference to the history of Babylon, and that he, Oscar, was exceedingly good at examinations. He asked Paul whether he had a private study, by any chance, and whether he were good at examinations. Paul replied evasively and asked whether he might peer down the microscope.

On the way home, Paul gathered some herbage for the Flemish Giant, more by habit than design. Later, while he was cleaning out the hutch and replenishing it with food, he scarcely took any notice of the rabbit. He did not watch it eat, nor did he stroke its fur or talk to it. As soon as he had finished he ran into the house and climbed up to the attic.

This attic was a dusty little room overlooking the garden, where he was allowed to do as he liked. The ceiling was low and on two sides it sloped nearly to the floor. Big flakes of whitewash had fallen from the ceiling on to the bare boards; one of the window panes was broken; there was no furniture at all in the room but a broken chair, an old trunk and boxes of discarded toys. Nevertheless it was a pleasant, sunny place in summertime and the window commanded a good view of trees, and tile roofs and chimney-pots beyond.

Paul, looking at the attic with an imaginative eye, could see the end wall bright with multi-coloured book jackets, a soft carpet on the floor, and a mahogany desk in the middle, upon which lay a brass microscope and papers relating to the history of Babylon, or some such place. And he could see himself as a dignified and reserved young man, furnished with a pair of horn-rimmed spectacles, writing feverishly by the light of an oil lamp.

He made a brief note in his diary recording the tea party at Mrs. Pimgrove's, and added underneath, in a peculiar code of his own invention, the words: Put away childish things. He completed the entry by inscribing an ornamental tailpiece whose cryptic meaning was For ever and ever.

The next day, the fourteenth day of the Flemish Giant's residence in the garden, was one of fasting for the rabbit. By midday it had eaten every particle of greenstuff in the hutch and every oat grain that it could find in the sawdust on the floor. Towards dusk it began to nibble the hay bedding.

Meanwhile Paul, full of energy and frowning with concentration, was busy in the basement making a desk. Plenty of old shelves were stacked there, and a box of nails and tools in plenty lay on the carpenter's bench. Paul grudged every moment spent in sleeping and washing and eating, got up early, asked to be excused from the table before anyone but he had finished, and worked in the evening till he was forcibly removed to his bedroom. Half the night he lay awake planning.

In the morning he bribed the maid to help him carry the desk from the basement to the attic. It looked a forlorn, shoddy desk compared with Oscar's, but a coat of white paint worked wonders, and the attic began really to resemble a study.

During tea-time Paul suddenly remembered the Flemish Giant. His conscience pricked him as he thought of the rabbit fasting while he feasted on unlimited quantities of ham and tongue and salad. Paul reserved some lettuce leaves for his pet, fetched some oats from the basement, and walked down to the bottom of the garden, feeling very guilty.

At first, not caring to look the Flemish Giant in the face, he stuffed the leaves through the wire mesh, keeping his eyes averted. When he saw the creature's back, however, and observed it was as plump as usual, he remembered that his mother had once told him that an occasional fast was good for everybody, and he felt quite happy again. He opened the door and tickled the rabbit's neck, as though to reassure it that ample supplies would not be wanting. To Paul it seemed that the Flemish Giant looked at him with forgiving eyes and made little gestures in thankfulness for the food. He patted it tenderly on the head and ran back to his study, resolving to give the rabbit one bumper meal a day, which it could either gobble up at once or eat at proper intervals, like a rational creature.

One by one, all the appurtenances of comfort and scholarship were installed in the attic. No obstacle held Paul up for long. What things he could not make out of the junk that lay in the cellar he borrowed from other rooms, wheedling them out of his mother, who was too weary and poor in health to resist him indefinitely; what he could not find in the house he cajoled her into letting him buy; what, even with his increased allowance, he could not afford, he contrived a substitute for. If there still remained some object which he could not by any means obtain, then he stoutly denied that it was necessary.

"Who wants a microscope to study the history of Babylon with?" he asked himself.

The bookshelves were easily framed out of planks. His own library filled the top shelf, and upon the others he put all those books which had been thrown contemptuously into boxes and placed in the cellar — musty volumes of the Home Almanac dating from the year 1880, Greek lexicons alive with fast-running book-lice that he spent hours exterminating, ponderous theological works whose pages had never been cut, catalogues of garden seeds and fishing tackle—anything, in fact, to fill the shelves. Chairs, wherever they seemed to be redundant, were taken up to the attic, and the maid's bedroom lost a hearth rug. A vase of flowers, the telephone which looked well but communicated with no one but the servant next door, papers and pens and inkpots in abundance, were among the furnishings. At the end of all his labours the study was comparable with Oscar's.

Paul began to brood in silence at mealtimes, to arch his fingers and frown. When someone addressed him he would not hear at first, then he would slowly raise his head and say, with a faraway look in his eyes, "Did you say something?" His voice bore a faint resemblance to the melancholy, detached tones of Oscar Pimgrove. At the end of a meal he would solemnly announce:

"I have certain matters to attend to in my study and would rather not be disturbed, if you please."

Neither the boys who called with invitations to cricket and country rambles, nor the friends of the family who offered to take him to the seaside in their cars, could drag him away from his desk. He had discovered a book about the history of Jerusalem—it was necessary to be that much different from Oscar. Even the sea had no glamour for him. He sent word to people that he was 'engaged.'

On the third day after the tea party Paul visited the Flemish Giant. He found the rabbit apparently quite happy, hopping about and nibbling at the last shreds of greenstuff that Paul had given it on the previous day. Paul emptied a bag of oats into the hutch and piled a heap of artichoke leaves and grass in one corner. He could not spare the time to clean out the hutch, which was beginning to smell unpleasantly. He would have more time tomorrow, he told himself.

During the four days that followed this visit, Paul was absorbed in the task of covering the backs of catalogues with pieces of wallpaper of various colours so that they might look bright and new in his bookcase, and in other improvements about the study. Once at night, when he lay in bed, he remembered the rabbit in the garden.

A pang of remorse troubled him for a moment before he fell asleep again. But the next morning proved so exciting—it was then that he bought a 'microscope' with one lens and examined hairs and cloth and book-lice beneath it—that the thought of the Flemish Giant was pushed to the back of his mind.

But Paul did not forget utterly about the rabbit. He was aware—uncomfortably aware—that he ought to be doing something. By some trick of the mind he contrived, half consciously, to prevent that thing appearing in the forefront of his thoughts. It was as though he remembered to forget.

On the fourth day he sat in his study reading the History of the Jewish War. In the garden the birds were singing as though they were half asleep, the curtains of ivy hanging outside the window pattered lazily against the glass, the room was oppressively hot. The press of manual work was over and Paul's mind, wandering from the study and from Titus' army and the siege of Jerusalem, alighted inevitably upon the Flemish Giant.

For a moment he felt a weight about his chest as though he were on the verge of tears. But he did not cry. He sat staring blankly at the page before him for ten minutes, without reading a word. He remembered the unpleasant condition of the hutch four days ago, and conjectured all-too-vividly its present state. He reckoned how long the provisions had lasted—a day and a half at the most. The image of the Flemish Giant, with its enlarged mournful, meek eyes, with its hip bones, always prominent, become dreadfully so, with its little sniffing nose moving constantly up and down in search of things to eat, drove everything else from his mind.

Paul got up and went to the window. Beyond the long lawn and the upturned soil of the kitchen garden, he could see the clump of artichokes, thick and green like a miniature copse, that hid the hutch from view.

Two or three times he started to go downstairs, returning each time to the window. It was too late, he thought. If only he had remembered it a day earlier... Now he could not bear to go. If the rabbit had been a fierce vindictive creature that hated him, then he would have gone. But the Flemish Giant was so mild and companionable. Paul felt the weight about his chest again when he thought of the rabbit's nose and its beautiful blue fur.

Then he tried to persuade himself that the Flemish Giant was already dead. The hope comforted him a little, though he knew it to be vain. With a great effort he started to read again, but at the end of the page he realized that he not grasped the meaning of one word. To divert his mind Paul went downstairs to the drawing room where his mother lay on the sofa, and sat with her. They talked for a while about Paul's school and other indifferent matters, but every now and then he would cease talking, rest his head on his hands and look very miserable.

Later in the day he ventured as far as the end of the lawn, and stood looking at the artichoke clump. He fancied he could see a swarm of flies over the spot where the hutch stood. He went back to the attic and for the rest of the day sat at his desk idle, staring at the same page till it was dusk.

Gradually, as the days went by, he became happier again. He spent two or three days at the seaside, and played cricket matches with his friends. For his birthday his uncle gave him a new three-spring bat. Soon the study became dusty and sprinkled with whitewash flakes once more, the mat was returned to the maid's bedroom, and there was no shortage of chairs about the house. Paul's conversation consisted of descriptions of his leg-break bowling and the number of runs he had scored on the previous afternoon. Once, when the name of Oscar Pimgrove was mentioned, he snorted with contempt and cried:

"What, that fusty old bookworm!"

One day in the early autumn Paul announced his intention of lighting a bonfire at the bottom of the garden. Cautiously, so as to avoid having to look through the wire netting, he approached the hutch from the rear, piled paper and wood between the brick supports, and struck a match.

Then he went up to his dusty, depleted study and stood by the window, watching clouds of smoke rise from the artichoke bed.

The smoke was almost the same colour as the fur of the Flemish Giant had been.

* * *

Chapter 4

Beetles

He had drawn a picture of a sexton beetle in his exercise book during the algebra lesson, and the master had caught him in the act. Five boys, one holding each arm and leg, and one holding down his head, had pinioned him during the beating. Afterwards, for a quarter of an hour, he had sat with his head buried in his hands, and then the master had drawn from the lapel of his coat a pin, had crept up behind and pricked him, while the boys tittered.

And now, school over, Manuel walked away towards the water meadows. His sobs became less convulsive and less frequent as he began to look about him. A little ahead, through a gap in the hedge, lay the field where the cows had been grazing. He crawled underneath the barbed wire and sat down beside a big heap of cow dung, and, taking a small stick and some matchboxes out of his pocket, began to look for the dung-beetles.

A crust baked to toughness by several days of sunshine covered the mound, like the crust of a loaf of bread; inside, the manure was soft and moist, a green-brown compost, tunnelled into a warren of chambers and corridors by the beetles. As he prodded the richly stinking mass with his stick they appeared, each dung-eater at the end of his food tunnel. Unbelievably clean and polished they seemed, most of them with bright black wing cases and carapaces, some dull and warty, and a few like nodules of lustrous metal. They scurried away and were lost in the grass; or, feigning death, stayed motionless for a little while, then made a stealthy dash for cover.

Soon the inhabitants of the heap were all either lost or captured and his attention turned to the grass around him. The earth was teeming. A green spider with delicate hairy legs hung lazily from a grass blade; two fierce brown ants zigzagged frantically among the stems beneath; a fly with an abdomen of blazing red tinfoil settled for a moment on his coat sleeve, then vanished in a flash. From under a fragment of the scattered dung a devil's coach-horse beetle appeared, holding aloft her black belly, and withdrew. The ragworts, rising sheer from the close-cropped grass, were stripped almost to nakedness by yellow-banded Cinnabar caterpillars. The pulsing air was noisy with the chirping of grasshoppers and the drone of the busy greenbottle flies, that are never languid even on the hottest day.

Between the stems of two ragworts stretched a web, almost invisible save for glistening beads of moisture where the threads met, of a great garden spider. Manuel, with his eye on the spider hiding under the leaves, threw a fragment of grass into the web. Immediately the fat creature rushed forward, seized the obstacle, and by a series of cunning motions pulled it clear of the sticky threads and cast it clean away. Then an unwary greenbottle became entangled and, struggling violently, tore a gap in the web. More cautiously the spider approached, let float her threads till they bound the fly in a strait-jacket of silk, then she pounced upon it, smothering it in her bulky embrace. As the jaws sunk into the body Manuel thought he could hear the flesh crackle like the rending of tissue paper. The convulsions of the fettered pain-stricken fly, and the spider working upon its body with a fearful insistence, roused his memory with a jerk.

Yes! In the midst of the turmoil he had for one second forgotten the whistle of the cane, the suppressed eager mirth of the boys who held him, the pain. For one moment the master had laid a hand on the back of his head—a gentle friendly hand, almost a comforting hand, yielding no pain. Yet the other was mobile, cunning in its task of inflicting harm, terribly intent upon the injury of his flesh. As with raised hand and hammer the workman bruises the wood, so the master seemed like an artisan, taking pleasure in the exercise of his craft. There was a great mystery in the difference between those two hands. And the preparation and the delay, the deliberate choice of the boys who were to hold him, the face of the master as he took off his coat and dealt a few preliminary swishes in the air—they too were fascinating and terrible. That night, he promised himself, he would borrow his mother's hand-mirror and look at the weals. Ten of them, blue and purple shaded; later they would pale to a greenish hue, and in a week or so only the memory of them would remain. He thought of the master, whose body could feel pain and show disfigurement also. How often he had thought of that—the master must one day suffer bodily anguish, die and rot away! How often he had pictured himself towering over the master, handling gently the hands that he would presently pierce with the nails, touching the feet before crossing them to drive the iron home, choosing carefully those who were to hold him down, delaying and making arrangements, talking with the victim while he, Manuel, wielded the hammer, and afterwards, as the master hung there, watching his face and showing him the scars of the beating!

A small brown head poked out of the end of a dung tunnel and drew back. But the boy had seen it, and seizing the stick, he thrust at the fragment here and there till the beetle appeared, large, round, slow-moving, encased in brilliant gold. The carapace shone like a jewel above the corrugated wing sheaths, which had a dimmer lustre; the legs were brown and stumpy, and the antennae, whose ends were flattened into little discs, waved with a regular motion. It was an unhurrying creature and unresentful. When Manuel held it between his fingers its limbs betrayed no sign of agitation, but rowed the air like little oars, slowly, with a sublime indifference. And on its back and belly and head there crawled a number of tiny parasites.

At home, an hour later, he took his matchboxes up to the bed-room. Beetles, he knew, were difficult to kill. For killing butterflies and moths he had used pounded laurel leaves, to the vapour of which butterflies soon succumbed. Moths lived longer. Sometimes a fat-bellied hawk-moth would survive for an hour in the laurel bottle, and beetles scarcely seemed to be affected at all. On one occasion, he remembered, a carrion beetle had spent an afternoon in the bottle and had emerged unscathed. In desperation he had cut off its head with a razor blade, intending to stick it on again afterwards, but the headless carcase had crawled away while he was looking for the glue.

Luckily, he reflected, cyanide of potassium is far more deadly than laurel leaves.

He emptied the matchboxes one by one into the new cyanide bottle. The last of them contained the gold beetle. It fell down on to the plaster surface with a thud and there it remained sprawling, with its legs waving in the air. The other beetles crawled over one another, ran round and round the base of the jar, or, attempting to climb the smooth sides, fell back repeatedly. For a long while, it seemed the beetles lived, but gradually the movements of the smaller ones grew weaker, then they rolled over and after a few tremors were still. But the golden beetle lived fully twice as long as any of the others.

Then came the pinning and the setting. The small black beetles were as tough as horn and crackled as he drove the pins through their right wing sheaths. Having fixed them in single file along a setting board, he arranged their legs and antennae with care, pulling them out with a needle. There they lay, a fine display of dung-eaters, stretching the length of the setting board, with legs extended like marchers frozen, yet still living. Their sheen, their vigorous rotundity, had suffered no change. Death seemed to touch them not at all. And like a king among them strode the golden beetle, cleaned of his parasites, as splendid in death as in life, save for the black pin through his belly.

That night Manuel lay with his head propped up on the pillows, admiring the beetles, wondering how it was that dung could turn itself into a nob of gold. As he wondered, the setting-board appeared green, dotted with mounds of cattle dung like pennies dropped here and there in the grass. And in the field walked a great beetle that wore a pair of silver horns. Over the gate it jumped in a twinkling, taking no more notice of it than if it had been a matchbox. Manuel crept up to the gate and peeped through into the field. The beetle had gone. There was nothing but snow everywhere and over the snow a blue-black sky with Chinese lanterns hanging down out of it, like emeralds and rubies. And there began a kind of music that he could not hear distinctly because the snow muffled it.

By this time the gate had grown so tall that he could not possibly jump over it. So he stood perfectly still and felt himself floating steadily upwards, while a crowd of children beneath clapped their hands and shouted hurray. Soon he could see the snow glittering on one side, and the children, no bigger than butterflies, dancing on the other. The air was motionless and full of gentle clangings that seemed to come from the Chinese lanterns. He waved goodbye to the children and sank, down, down, and down till his feet touched the snow.

In the distance there stood a church with a tall steeple, and red light glowing through the windows. Manuel could see the priest kneeling before an image of Jesus, made of wood and enamel. The people knelt down and the organ began to play, softly at first, then louder and louder, but with a hushed loudness, as the notes tumbled over one another in their race across the snow. Then the tenor bell in the steeple gave a great boom, the music ceased, the church vanished, and Manuel discovered that the snow beneath him was drifting away.

Again he stood perfectly still and wished. Soon he was sailing lightly above the clouds, while the sound of the children clapping below grew fainter, and died away. Up here the sun shone beautifully. Stretching far beneath were innumerable cloudlets that looked like white curling feathers mingled with rose petals. The air was fresher and more limpid than the purest breeze that ever blew over the lower earth. The sky was a richer blue, the sun a more brilliant yellow than he had ever known. He plunged till he reached the cloud tufts, then soared again into the blue. And all around him there was music, unspeakably clear and sweet. Then he started falling slowly, slowly, till at last he tumbled on to the snow again.

He sat there, numb with terror at what he saw. A golden beetle, about the size of a mouse, was creeping stealthily over the snow to where he was. Its face was the face of the master, contorted into an expression of diabolical merriment, and as black as the night. Horridly, and with mechanical deliberation it advanced, the motion of each leg like the stab of a little bayonet. Manuel could not move, could not wink an eyelid. When he tried to call out, no sound came from his throat. Great beads of blood gathered on his forehead and, dripping on the snow, stained it crimson. Then the thing touched him, mounted his foot, and began to climb his leg, each claw rasping the skin and leaving a long blue wound. Higher and higher it climbed, becoming larger at each step, and glowing fearfully. For a moment it stood still on his thigh. Then he screamed and woke.

He found himself sitting up in the bed, naked. A ray of faint starlight shone across his body, and there on his thigh sat the golden beetle, still impaled on the pin, shimmering, with its horns in a tremble. Then it strode forward, scraping his flesh with the pin, till it toppled over and fell into the bed.

The spell broken, Manuel leaped on to the floor, shaking violently. Meanwhile there came from the direction of the table a scratching sound, and he went across to look. In the dim light he saw the setting board and the row of beetles, all of them come to life again, scraping at the paper with their legs. One of them rode up and down on its pin like a rider in the saddle, and around the pin there oozed from the beetle's body a globule of moisture. From the setting board, across the table and along the sheet ran a little trail of blood, left by the golden beetle.

He picked it up by its pin from the bed, pinned it again to the setting board, and sat down to watch. Until sunrise he sat at the table, too absorbed to feel the cold.

For two days the beetles lived, then one by one grew weaker and came to rest. But the golden beetle lived on, riding up and down on its pin, scraping two grooves in the board with its legs. Every day, after school was over, Manuel sat watching it, and on the evening of the third day it died.

* * *

Chapter 5

The Bird Of Paradise

There were two shops in the village of Bricett Combust—the Post Office, which was kept by Mr Blowers and Mrs Blowers, and the Old Shop, which was kept by Miss Adele Pheby, a little woman with white hair and rosy cheeks.

The Post Office Shop was prosperous and the old one wasn't. But in times gone by it had been the other way round. Before the post and telegraph were set up in Bricett Combust, Mr Blowers had served the children with licorice strips and acid drops, farthing transfers and crayons, fireworks and toffee apples, but he used not to go in for solid, respectable goods like flour and bacon and bread and tea, at least, not to any extent; and never on any account did he serve the gentlefolk—the Vaspers up at the Hall and the Vicar's wife. In the old days Miss Pheby had done that; it was she who had the solid, respectable goods on her counter and ranged neatly on her shelves; it was her door bell that was constantly clanging with the coming and going of customers—customers that were worth having, mark you, who bought great packages of groceries on a Saturday and odd things during the week, customers that bought regular and paid regular, and some of them gentles too.

Miss Pheby used to sigh again and again when she thought about it all. Not that she had sunk altogether to the level of bullseyes and clear fruit gums. Oh dear no! The baker still left her four or five loaves a day, which she kept in a new dustbin that was also for sale; there was still a row of cannisters with the remains of gilt letters on them and a little tea, and snuff, and rice and such-like inside. And you could still buy a packet of butter from her, or a cake of soap, or even a hat if you wanted to. But though Miss Pheby would much rather make you a present of something than sell you anything that she was certain wasn't quite fresh and nice, you really couldn't count on her. As like as not her fireworks were last year's and utterly incapable of exploding, her bread the day before yesterday's and

47

as dry as old boots, and her shag and her twist, Lord knows how dusty and ancient! The only girl that had bought a hat at the Old Shop for the last five years was Cissy Midler, and everyone knew that she wasn't quite right. The hat was a pre-war creation, a huge thing, full of ferns and feathers, with an artificial bird of paradise in the middle and the moth in it besides. Every week for years Miss Pheby had dusted it with a feather brush, blown out the dirt that had gathered in its dark undergrowth, and put it back on its stand. Then Cissy had come in and tried it on in front of the mirror, bought it for a shilling, and had ever since worn it on Sundays. Miss Pheby had another hat just like it, except that it had the moth rather more badly. Her only hope of selling it, even for ninepence, was that Cissy would wear hers out one day and buy this one instead. That was the only chance, because no other girl in Bricett Combust could be expected to wear a hat like Cissy's. In her more abandoned moods Miss Pheby contemplated the possibility of wearing the hat herself, when she went to church on a Sunday. But directly she remembered the serious state of trade she gave up the idea of such a piece of frivolity.

Trade was indeed slow, but then, it might have been worse. Fortunately the Old Shop was at one end of the village, the Post Office was at the other, and the village street was a long one, so that when folks at Miss Pheby's end were in a hurry for something, or when it was raining hard, they didn't bother to traipse all the way to Mr Blowers'. The Parson always bought his tobacco, which Miss Pheby got in specially, from the Old Shop, and, as everybody remarked, it smoked like a chimney. And the children, not being so particular as their elders, patronized Miss Pheby more than they did Mr Blowers, who treated them curtly. Taking the thick with the thin, she managed to get along all right.

But she couldn't have done so without Miss Kate Pheby, her younger sister. Miss Kate went up to the Hall and the Vicarage on alternate days to do the cleaning. It wasn't a nice thing to do, after having been serving in her own shop for years and years, but it brought in, when you reckoned it up, more than the shop did. Another thing that helped was that the shop and the cottage, which were under the same roof, belonged to them, had been theirs since their father had died and left it to them twenty years ago. There wasn't any rent to pay and the rates were only a shilling or two a year.

Miss Pheby never grumbled, on the other hand she was not always contented. As she sat in her kitchen waiting for the shop bell to ring, she would sometimes desire to see something of the world. Once, when she was a girl, her father had taken her to the Big Town thirty miles away, and they had gone to the Play and the Fair.

O what a wonderful day that had been! She had treasured up every one of its golden moments in her mind, bringing them out from time to time for loving inspection like a miser. The old gipsy woman in the tent who had told her fortune—and what a fortune! The gay round-abouts with their uproarious music, and the big marquee full of animals—she saw them all as clear as noonday. She had ridden on the elephant and she had ridden on the camel. She had seen the man poke the porcupine with a broomstick to make the funny creature show its quills. She had seen a brave gentleman, dressed up as though he were about to be married, walk right into the lions' den and make the terrible creatures jump about and sit on boxes as if they had been no more frightful than so many kittens. And then, in the evening, they had gone to the theatre, which turned out to be better even than the menagerie. The play had been about a beautiful lady, more beautiful than an angel, Miss Pheby had thought; a wicked villain with great curling mustachios and oily hair; and a handsome young lover. The sufferings of the beautiful young lady at the hands of the villain, the flutterings of her heart when she met the lover under the moon in the orchard, the disasters that beset, while they could frustrate, the course of true love—all were felt as keenly by Miss Pheby as if she had been the beautiful young lady herself. On the way home in the train Miss Pheby wouldn't talk to anyone, for fear of breaking the spell. For several days after she tried, desperately and with waning success, to feel and behave like the noble young lady in the play. But it was no good doing that in a place where everyone knew her, and her friends couldn't be expected to understand, not having been to the play. Gradually she had fallen back into the old ways. All the same she felt that since the Play life had been different.

That all happened thirty five years ago, and she hadn't even seen the inside of a railway train since. In all the intervening years she hadn't been further afield than Bury St. Edmunds, on a motor bus, and even that had been a big event. Now she was growing old; she hadn't much more than ten or fifteen years to live perhaps, and she wanted to go to the Big Town again, to the Fair and the Play once more before she died. For several years this desire had grown in her till it filled her thoughts almost to the exclusion of everything else. Even in church her attention would wander from the service and she would contemplate the elephant and the porcupine that she had seen at the Fair. Hitherto the singing of the choir and the organ music had filled her with joy; now in her imagination it became the incidental music while the lovers in the Play held hands.

Every week Miss Pheby put something by, if it was only a penny, and though it often meant going to bed at eight o'clock to save candle-light. At the end of the two years she had twenty shillings in the toffee tin that she kept in the old Dutch oven in the kitchen. It was enough, more than enough, to go to the town with, and it would pay for the Fair and the Play. Nevertheless Miss Pheby was not at all sure that she would go, after all. She felt quite afraid of the Big Town. She had heard that it had changed, grown, become more frightening and wonderful.

For one thing, Kate couldn't go with her. Kate, who could easily get a day off from her cleaning, would have to look after the shop, in Miss Pheby's absence. It would be alarming to go all by herself, amongst all those smart, clever, perhaps unfriendly people. Yet the Play and Fair — ah, they would be worth it!

Then, one day in November, it was all decided, as it were, for her. That morning, Miss Pheby began by dusting all the things on the shelves in the shop — a job that hadn't been necessary in the old days. She was wearing an apron made out of an old sugar sack, with the edges nicely hemmed, and a black dress with a lace collar that stood out stiffly like a ruff, very neat and prim. Though the shop was not much more than six feet high she had to stand on a chair to get at the top shelves. Packed with all sorts of things were these shelves — rat traps that were sadly rusted, finger marked cards with pens and pencils tied to them, water pistols that would no longer hold water, small iron bombs and boxes of pink caps to go with them, bags of marbles and glass-alleys, and much else. She took them out one by one, flicked them with her feather brush and put them back. After she had finished the top shelf, which ran round three sides of the shop, Miss Pheby sat down, quite tired out with her effort.

So far, and it was already half past ten in the morning, nobody at all had come into the shop. That, she reflected, was because it was such a pleasant day, very sunny and warm for November, and people would be going to Mr Blowers' down the road. She looked between the sweet bottles and out of the window. Just opposite the shop, in the meadow, grew a splendid mountain ash. Now it was full of scarlet berries. She watched the bunches of berries swishing in the breeze and sparkling when the sun fell on them.

Presently the tooting of a car interrupted the silence and a smart saloon drew up outside the window, with a great squeaking of brakes. Miss Pheby stood up behind the counter. It wasn't often that cars stopped outside the shop.

The door opened, making the bell ring furiously, and a gentleman walked in. He was a handsome young man in a bowler and blue coat, and he wore wash-leather gloves. He reminded Miss Pheby of the lover in the Play. But he wasn't a customer, alas — Miss Pheby knew him well — he was a commercial traveller who sold tins of salmon.

"Good mornin' sir," said Miss Pheby, who was polite, even to travellers.

"Morning ma'am," said the young man, taking off his hat and laying it on the counter. "And how many salmons do you want today?

Ah," he said, leaning forward and gazing at Miss Pheby intently, "I have a wonderful line in lobsters today, scrumptious they are." He smacked his lips.

Miss Pheby was quite sure that she didn't want any lobsters, or salmon either. On the other hand she didn't like to say so outright.

She smiled at the young man and said,

"Trade be that bad I don't rightly know as I want anything."

"Come, come, Miss Pheby. I tell you they're scrumptious. People will queue for them." Before she could correct him there came another ringing of the bell and a small boy with a runny nose trotted in and stood with his head projecting an inch above the counter.

"Scuse me a tick while I sarve the young man," said Miss Pheby.

"Two penny demons an' a pillar o' fi-er," said the boy, sniffing.

"Lordy, lordy," exclaimed Mr Bone, (that was the traveller's name) regarding the boy with astonishment.

Miss Pheby, being quite used to this kind of trade, found the fireworks in a cardboard tray and gave them to the boy, who ran out without a word.

"Them boys!" she said, after he had gone, "Howsomever, I do sell more o' them demons than what I do tins o' salmon. Tha' I do."

Mr Bone drew a card from his pocket and gave it to Miss Pheby.

"There's an invitation for you, Miss Pheby," he said.

Miss Pheby took it, found her spectacles somewhere on the counter, put them on and read:

Ideal Homes
F A I R
Exhibition Hall, November 3rd to 17th,
ADMIT BEARER
(Ticket value 1/-)
With the compliments of Messrs Tone.
Stand No. 146 - B

Miss Pheby could scarcely believe her eyes.

"For me?" she gasped.

"Certainly."

"Ah, but how should I git there, all the tharty mile an' more?"

"Supposing I was to take you in my car?"

Miss Pheby threw up her hands with astonishment.

"Will there be a porc'pine at the Fayer?"

Mr Bone scratched his head.

"There'll be our lobsters," he said.

"Or a elephant?"

"I doubt there'll be an elephant. But it's ever so interesting all the same."

Miss Pheby looked disappointed.

"Will there be a play at the theaytre?"

"O rather. Bound to be."

"I'll come. O yes I'll come," she said, quivering with excitement.

After that she had to order a few tins of salmon.

Miss Pheby thanked the traveller with all her heart and off he drove in the big car, the same that was going to take her to the Big Town!

That was on a Friday, and Mr Bone had arranged to pick her up on the following Tuesday. On Friday night and the nights that followed, Miss Pheby scarcely slept a wink, she was so thrilled. At church she didn't sing at all, and even forgot to stand up at the proper times. She told everyone that came into the shop about the excursion and had a long talk with the Vicar about it. She asked him if he thought it was quite right that she should go to the Fair and the Play.

"Why yes, Miss Pheby," he said. "Twill do you a heap of good."

"I don't say as I aint a tiny bit afeared o' such a tarble big place," she confided to him.

"O you'll be all right," said the Vicar kindly.

On Monday night Miss Pheby took down the bird of paradise hat from its stand, carried it into the kitchen and sat by the fire, with the hat on her lap. She blew some of the dust off it and began to sew a length of violet ribbon round the edge.

Her sister Kate, a big woman with a placid face, was sitting in the chair opposite, with her hands folded in her lap, gazing into the fire. Miss Pheby sewed in silence. Presently she said, in her tiny shrill voice,

"I do wish you was a comen too, Kate."

"I'll bide by the shop," said Kate.

"Do you go stead o' me."

"No feyer. 'T'was allus been your wish ter go, an' I'll bide by the shop."

Miss Pheby's hands were a little trembly as she sewed. Every now and then she regretted having been so impetuous, and a kind of shiver would pass through her.

After a while Kate went up to bed. When the hat was finished Miss Pheby tried it on in front of the mirror. It was enormous, and her little face looked quite lost under such a mass. The bird of paradise sat perched in the middle with its perky little head cocked to one side and its glass eyes gleaming mischievously in the candle-light. All round it there surged a sea of black and white, an indescribable ocean of feathers and lace and artificial leaves. The hat was more like a depressed busby, broken out into monstrous blossom, than any ordinary head-gear. But Miss Pheby's face glowed with pleasure at the sight. She took it off at last and went to bed.

Next morning punctually at ten o'clock Mr Bone came for her, and there were several people outside to see them start. Miss Pheby had ransacked the cottage and found an ancient boa, which nearly enveloped her face, and made her resemble the bird of paradise even more closely. She carried an umbrella with a bone handle and a large bag made of American cloth, containing sandwiches. Having kissed her sister goodbye on the doorstep, she clambered into the car, too overcome to say a word to the people who wished her good luck. Everyone waved and shouted encouraging things and off they drove.

It was a beautiful ride, though at first Miss Pheby was scared to death. Every time Mr Bone took a corner she clutched the seat and was sure that they would be killed. But Mr Bone was a clever driver and got round somehow. After a while Miss Pheby sat back comfortably and put her trust in him. At first she was more interested in the knobs and levers, that Mr Bone manipulated with such skill, than in the country. Then she looked out of the window. The countryside was bathed in a soft watery sunlight. The leaves hadn't all fallen yet, and some of the trees shone a beautiful golden brown against the blue haze in the distance. When they passed through a village, Miss Pheby would look at the people and straighten herself up. The bird of paradise flopped about a little with the jolting of the car, making her feel rather awkward, but it was grand to be riding in a private car with such a gentlemanly looking driver as Mr Bone, and all the folks looking on!

After a long time they came to the streets of the Big Town. Miss Pheby stared aghast at the rushing tramcars, the gigantic buildings, the throngs of people all dressed up to the nines (as she told Kate afterwards), and the traffic that made her head swim — all so different from what she remembered. Mr Bone set her down opposite the Exhibition Hall, gave her a lot of instructions about what to do, how to see the Fair, where to eat her dinner, and how to get to the theatre, which all went in one ear and out of the other, she was so flurried. When he had left her she wanted to run after him and ask for his protection. However, since that was impossible, she walked straight up the grand staircase into the Hall.

It was a vast building, so much bigger than the Church at Bricett Combust that it made her feel something like an ant on a barnfloor. Miss Pheby wandered timidly down a gangway lined with exhibition stands, looking for cages full of animals. All she could see were pianos and chairs and electric cleaners and things of that sort — it was nothing at all like a Fair! As soon as she stopped and looked at some curious bit of machinery, or at a sweet stall that seemed quite like home, a dreadfully smart gentleman would pounce out of a den where he had been hiding all the time, and start asking her to buy something. After this had happened three or four times Miss Pheby became flustered and almost ran down the gangway, without looking to left or right.

Then she spied an arch of roses leading to a patch of green that reminded her of her own garden. Through the arch she went and found a lawn, with a border of delightful flowers and a lake in the middle and a gravel path running round it with seats—all as if it had been in the country itself, except for the noise. Even the noise—noises of engines clanking, people shouting, a band playing somewhere—was a little less here. Miss Pheby sat down on one of the benches and sighed. She looked at the flowers and the grass and wondered however they managed to grow in such a place. But just as she was comfortably settled an objectionable, foreign looking man with a fat stomach waddled up to her and said,

"Allow me to interest you in our seed, modom."

Miss Pheby snatched up her bag and fled.

For an hour she wandered round the exhibition, without any peace or rest, without having glimpsed so much as a bird, let along any strange animal. All the while she was getting more and more tired and distraught, and the people were looking at her in a funny sort of way.

Then, as she was passing a pen nib stall, a man darted out and pushed a little box containing a fountain pen into her hand. She was about to give it back to him, when the man said with a smile,

"It's free. Advertisement, madam. Free gift."

Miss Pheby murmured her thanks and immediately felt encouraged at the friendliness of the man.

"Ah, but you'll need some nibs to go with it, wont you?" he said, producing four yellow nibs in a box.

"Course I will!" said Miss Pheby, delighted with the man's generosity.

"Gold plated madam. One and six each, to go with the pen."

Miss Pheby's face fell. She tried to protest, but before she could find her voice the man said,

"That will be six shillings."

Her hands trembled as she fished about in her bag for the money.

After that was over she found a chair and sat down, utterly exhausted. Tears filled her eyes when she reckoned how long it had taken to save those six shillings. She wanted to take the wretched pen — what should she want with a fountain pen, indeed — and throw it at the man. Instead she just sat still while her legs recovered, and resolved not to look at or listen to anyone or anything till she got safely out of the building.

Outside, the streets, busy as they were, seemed restful by comparison. By midday she had found her way to the Cathedral. How beautiful it was in there, and how quiet after the roar of the Exhibition Hall! How friendly and soothing, with no one to pester the life out of her! Miss Pheby sat down in one of the pews and stared up at the great vault, hanging there miraculously like a sky of stone, and at the sturdy pillars that looked as though they had been there since the creation of the world. The sunlight came in the upper windows and slanted down to the floor in thin, dusky yellow rays, full of dancing motes. Beyond the great screen that divided the Presbytery from the Nave, she could see the vault going on and on as though there were no end to it. Presently the organ began to play, now sweetly with little trilling treble notes which made her think of the rippling reflections thrown by sunlit water, now grandly with the ponderous bass, that was so solemn and comforting. There were very few people in the Cathedral and none of them took any notice of Miss Pheby, which was just what she wanted. After all, she was glad she had come.

After half an hour she felt hungry, so she undid her packet of cheese sandwiches and started to nibble them secretly, in order that no one should see her eating in a Church...

All the afternoon she sat in the Cathedral, quite still. There was a short service, with such singing as she had never heard in all her life, so sweet and clear it was, and more playing of the organ. Then gradually, as the light faded, and the great arches grew indistinct with shadows, the Cathedral became quite deserted and silent. Miss

Pheby knelt down, and remained kneeling for some time. Then she went out, feeling refreshed and cheerful, to find the theatre.

When she got there she found that she had a long while to wait till the theatre doors opened. So she sat down on some steps and watched all the sights of the city. It was dark now, and the street lamps and the shop windows were ablaze. Miss Pheby, sitting in the shadow of the doorway, could see everything—the huge white fronts of the buildings, the cars tearing past, the townsfolk decked up in their evening clothes, the bawling newsboys—without being seen herself. The time didn't hang heavily at all.

At seven o'clock the theatre doors were opened, and she found the gallery door. Up an interminable staircase that went round and round she climbed and bought a ticket from a man sitting in a kind of cage, then up more stairs and into the gallery itself. She got a seat right at the edge, where she could look over the rail into the pit.

As yet the theatre was nearly empty. It didn't look anything like the theatre of her memory, but it was very grand. Enormous dusty ladies and fat little boys with gilt hair and gilt wisps of raiment like ribbons lolled against the ceiling in dangerous attitudes, quite near to where she sat. She regarded them for a long time with awe, and some surprise at their nakedness. Then she looked over the rail, down into the theatre, which was shaped like a chimney. Over the boxes there were more ladies and boys on prancing steeds, and lots of gilded and blue filigree work; and the opening of the stage was wonderful to see, a riot of ornaments around the rich plush curtain. And right down in the pit, an incredible distance below, were the people coming in and taking their seats—beautifully dressed ladies and men dressed in black like undertakers. Miss Pheby was entranced.

Then the orchestra came in through a little door underneath the stage and began to play, while more and more people came in. Soon the pit was dotted all over with heads, like pins in a pin-cushion. Miss Pheby looked round and saw that the gallery was filling too. Hundreds of faces were ranged behind her and on either side, looking, as you might say, at her. It was rather embarrassing, so she turned round again quickly. On one side of her there was a fat little man eating peanuts and on the other there were three young fellows, cracking jokes and letting balls of silver paper fall into the pit, aiming them at an old gentleman's bald head. Miss Pheby thought they were very rude, but she leaned over too, to see where the silver paper went.

She didn't see where it went to, but she saw something much stranger than that. A little brown thing, a bird, was floating in the air, fluttering and falling down and down into the pit as though it were very tired. Miss Pheby wondered how the poor thing had got into the theatre, and whether it were hurt. Everyone was watching it and seemed to be very amused at such a thing. There was a lot of laughter and some shouting. Finally the bird lighted on the lap of the bald old gentleman, who sprang from his seat with astonishment and looked up at the gallery. The boys next to Miss Pheby were roaring with laughter, while the fat man was holding his stomach as though it were threatening to burst, and making noises in his throat. Presently, amid the noise, Miss Pheby heard someone behind say,

"Look at your hat!"

She was bewildered. There had been something familiar about that bird... But no, it couldn't be!... Still came the cries, "Look at your hat."

Miss Pheby turned round and saw that everyone in the gallery was looking at her, and some of them were pointing at her hat and laughing.

She went quite crimson and trembled, not knowing what to do. The fat man gurgled something about taking off her hat and looking at it.

With some difficulty she drew out the long pins that passed through the lace undergrowth and into the bun of her hair, and took off the hat. The bird of paradise was gone.

Grasping her bag and umbrella in one hand and her hat in the other, she stumbled up the gallery, past all the people, and somehow got down the stairs and out into the street, where she sat down on the steps weeping.

Very soon a theatre attendant came running along with the bird in his hand.

"Here you are, lady," he said, giving it to her. "Don't take it so hardly, lady," he added, in a kind voice, "It might 'ave 'appened to anyone."

She thanked him very much and took the bird and put it in her bag. He helped her to get herself straight again and then suggested that she should go back and see the play.

But Miss Pheby refused point blank. She would wait for Mr Bone outside.

When at last Miss Pheby got back to Bricett Combust, all her longing for the Big Town, with its Fair and its Theatre, had gone. The only memory of it that she cherished was of the Cathedral. In church on Sundays she no longer thought about the lovers in the Play or the elephant and porcupine, but followed every note of the singing and every word of the sermon.

And she sewed the bird of paradise onto the hat again with some strong packing thread, and put it back on its stand, where it remained, becoming more and more dusty and moth-eaten every year, till she died and the shop was sold. Then it was thrown in the dustbin.

* * *

Chapter 6

The Stink

It was a grim cold pile, more like a prison than a school, built of drab grey bricks. The bleak mountain of buildings stood in the centre of a plain of asphalte, a sere desert more gloomy even than the grey walls. In this waste land we played 'ship-a-sailing' and marbles and fought one another from time to time. Here too we marched, formed fours, and stood easy, to orders barked by the master. On Empire Day the whole school used to assemble in the desert and sing Rule Britannia while the Union Jack was hauled up the flagstaff, and elderly gentlemen stood in a bunch talking to the headmaster.

At one end of the playground was a block of lavatories which were always so foul that the more delicately nurtured boys would not go near the place except in the utmost need, and even the coarser fellows used to stand on the seats. Toilet paper was never seen. A cycle shed adjoined the place, and was used as a shelter. When it was wet we had to pack ourselves so tightly into the shed that we could hardly move, or remain outside in the rain.

Our classroom was a tall room, lit by long church-like windows. The walls were unplastered, so that long ridges of dust used to collect on the surface of the brickwork and the place had a comfortless look. Around the whitewashed walls ran a wooden dado, always decorated with a number of drawings by a boy called Copeman, who had gained the distinction of being the artist of the class by means of his peculiar method of shading, which he contrived by smudging the paper with his forefinger. In addition to Copeman's elaborately shaded drawings of spades and pails and brooms there was a portrait of King George as Prince of Wales, with a pair of flags floating over his head and a dreadnought underneath, supported on bright blue waves.

In front of the desks stood the teacher's table, a movable blackboard and, to one side, a large and evil-smelling slow-combustion stove, from which a twisting flue pipe, like some monstrous iron tree, mounted to the ceiling. The desks were continuous and arranged in tiers, each a step higher than the last, so that the room resembled a theatre, in which sixty boys were the audience and the master, as a rule, the sole actor.

We called him Screws—I have long forgotten his real name. He was thin and dark and electric. When he was in a good temper you scarcely dared to whisper or shuffle your feet; when he scowled at you, you were paralysed; when he was really angry existence seemed a crime. Boys in the other classes put hairs in the end of the master's cane in order to split it, and filled their inkwells with carbide; they made paper aeroplanes and flew them openly during lessons; they played tunes on pen nib points stuck in their desks. But Screws' boys were always good. They had to be.

Nevertheless Screws had a sense of humour. I well remember how, when I had failed hopelessly to learn the 23rd Psalm, he gave me a couple of hearty strokes with his cane and said with a devilish chuckle:

"My rod and my staff, they comfort you!"

But Screws was not always with us. There was an interval, for instance, between prayers and the morning's first lesson, when we were given some respite. One of these occasions is associated with my earliest memory of a boy whose name was Baster.

Some of us were standing round the stove (for it was a bitterly cold day), warming our hands and spitting on the ironwork to hear the moisture sizzle, and watch it froth and boil away. Baster was playing a game by himself with an improvised dart made of a pen nib broken short, aiming at a spot on the matchboarding which served as a bull's eye. Presently someone gave the word that Screws was on his way, and we all scampered for our seats.

As soon as Screws was inside the door he saw the pen nib dart sticking in the dado. He turned towards the boys, seated in silent rows.

"Whose is this?" he said, speaking between his teeth.

Nobody replied.

After several seconds he repeated the question.

Still there was no reply, only some meaningful glances at Baster. "Very well then," said Screws, "I shall cane the whole class."

I tried to get a glimpse of Baster's face from where I was sitting, but it was out of view. For some reason the hymn that we had sung that morning kept ringing in my head:

> "Jesus meek and gentle,
> Son of God most high,
> Pitying, loving Saviour,
> Hear thy children's cry."

I remembered Screws' face, black and inscrutable, and his powerful voice booming out the words.

A boy at the front of the class got up and blurted out:

"Please s'r, it's Baster's."

A scarcely audible flutter told the relief of the class. You had more than a sense of respite from Screws when a fellow was caught. It gave you a sense of well-being to think how lucky you were compared with the poor devil on the stage, while you were safe in the audience.

Screws unlocked his cupboard and took out his carefully preserved cane, saying to Baster:

"Come out and get your property then, Baster."

Baster went down the gangway between the desks irresolutely, though uncertain of where he was going. He walked round Screws, keeping as far away from his cane as possible, and pulled the dart out of the wall. Then he turned round and faced Screws.

Baster was not a lovely sight. Sticking out of his mouth were two large teeth, dominating his face. He looked hunted, as though he were trying to hide in the midst of his voluminous raglan jacket. He could not take his eyes away from Screws, who stood over him, smart and business-like, brandishing the cane.

"Hold out your hand."

Baster extended a grubby left palm.

As the cane descended Baster winced, drawing up his face till his eyes disappeared, and clenching his right hand.

"Now the right," said Screws.

After it was over Baster still stood there wringing his hands, pressing them together as though in supplication, then bending down and squeezing them between his knees to ease the pain. But he did not make a sound, or cry.

Baster began to walk back to his seat. Screws caught his shoulder and drew him back.

"Baster," he said with a grimace, "you stink."

Baster was too much occupied with his hands to take much notice.

"Has anyone else observed that Baster stinks?" asked Screws, addressing the class.

No one answered. As a matter of fact we had noticed Baster's odour. It was peculiar. He was certainly not the only boy in the class who stank. I believe I could have named half a dozen of them blindfold, each by his own smell. But Baster's was the most powerful and the most offensive. You could even distinguish a piece of paper that had been in Baster's pocket, if your sense of smell was acute enough, as mine was.

But Screws could get nothing out of the class about Baster's smell.

"Very well," he said, "we'll isolate you, Stinker. Sit over in the corner."

So Baster went back to his desk, got his pen and went to his new place at the back of the classroom, where he was some distance from the nearest boy.

After this affair Screws and most of the boys always referred to Baster as the Stinker, and to his corner of the room as Stinker's Corner.

Stinker's Corner soon became a new weapon in Screws' armoury.

"Stinker's corner for you," he would shout at a boy whose book was blotted and dirty.

I was often sent to sit next to Stinker, and so came to know him better, till we were almost friends. I say 'almost' because no one was ever really friendly with Baster. He was an unsociable fellow, with views of his own; he was what we called 'funny'. But this funniness, though it made our relations difficult, induced in me a sort of sympathy. I rather liked sitting next to Baster, in spite of his smell.

At intervals Baster told me something about his home life, most of which I have forgotten. All that I remember is that his father kept a little butcher's shop and was a good Templar.

This latter peculiarity of Baster senior's was destined to bring further trouble to his son, to strengthen the understanding that existed between us, and indirectly to lead to my discovery of his secret.

It happened that one day Baster saw one of the boys, Nichols was his name, fetching a mug of beer from a public house for his father's dinner. Baster delivered a lecture to Nichols about the shame of drunkenness and the evil effects of alcohol, to which Nichols could not effectively reply, being harassed with his burden. All he could do was to say:

"My dad may drink, but he don't stink," and swear an early revenge.

Vengeance fell heavily and soon upon Baster. The next morning before the school bell rang, Nichols gathered his cronies together in the cycle shed and told them of the insult and of his dad's war wounds, which, Nichols said, deserved the reward of an occasional mug of beer. His appeal had the desired effect, and it was agreed that vengeance should be wreaked that afternoon after school was over.

Such decisions were not kept secret for long amongst us. Before the day was out Baster had some idea of what was coming to him, and when four o'clock struck he was evidently worried. Since his seat was at the back and he would be one of the last boys to leave, he stood little chance of escape.

Nichols got to the playground gate first and collared Baster while he was trying to sneak through in the midst of the crowd. Presently Nichols' two friends arrived and helped to drag Baster back to a corner of the yard, where they held him till most of the boys had gone.

It had been decided that Nichols' friends should pin Baster against a wall while Nichols took a few 'running kicks' at him. Actually the revenge did not take so dignified a form, for Baster had plenty of fight in him. Nichols executed a running kick or two, but the kicks landed in the wrong places and hurt the wrong boys. Then 'bumping' was tried. They held Baster by his hands and feet and dropped him on the paving.

But this method was not entirely successful, and the affair degenerated into a rough-and-tumble in which Baster was usually underneath and Nichols on top, sitting on Baster's belly and pounding away at whatever portions of the scrimmage seemed to belong to Baster. Certainly he stood no chance against three boys, each as big as himself. For five minutes he squirmed and fought, not so much against the feeble blows directed at him as against the oppressive weight of the boys.

At last everyone had had enough and Baster was released. When he got up he was pale and very near to tears. But he repressed them, found his cap, and began to run away home.

The revenge, however, was not yet complete. Baster had not cried, though he was obviously about to do so. Accordingly his three enemies ran after him to see whether he would break down, and I followed to see what would happen. After a long chase we caught up with him in a blind alley and cornered him.

He turned and faced us there. The tears were flowing fast now, streaming down his dirty cheeks, and his face was distorted with sobbing.

"Look at him crying," the boys shouted, laughing.

"Look at old stink pot."

Baster tore off his cap and covered his face with it, while I begged them to stop.

"You've had your vengeance," I said.

One of them went up to Baster, sniffed at him, and retired holding his nose.

"Pooh, what a stink!" he cried, still holding his nose.

I said again that they had done enough.

With this they appeared to agree, and they went off home.

Baster soon recovered and we walked home together. It was then, as a reward for what little I had done for him, that he promised to let me into his secret.

The next afternoon, after school was over and I had promised faithfully never to tell a soul of what I was about to see, he took me to see his bodies.

The first was behind a gate that led to a coal merchant's yard. With an air of great mystery we concealed ourselves between the open gate and the wall of the yard, and Baster lifted an old newspaper, revealing what looked to me like a dead rat, in whose hairy skin white maggots were crawling. As I watched, I noticed one of them poke its head out of the creature's ear. The smell was the smell of Stinker, grown more powerful.

We turned the body over and looked at the underside. Here a mass of wriggling maggots were feeding on the loosening flesh. The rats mouth was open and full of the things.

Baster bent down and examined the carcass minutely, pushing at the flesh with the butt of a pencil and squashing some of the maggots.

"She's getting on nicely," he said with a pleased look, when he had finished.

"How d'you mean?" I asked, failing to understand.

"Wait and you'll see," replied Baster.

Then we ran through the back streets of the town for a quarter of a mile till we came to a piece of waste ground, where rubbish had been dumped in heaps. We clambered over mounds of cinders and old cans and found a place that Baster had marked by pushing a stick in the ground. There, concealed in a hollow place, was a creature that might once have been a cat. Now it was a shapeless mass, all greenish and burrowed by crawling things and stinking horribly.

But Baster was evidently delighted at the state of the carcass. He turned it over reverently, but in spite of his care the side of the animal stuck to the cinders, revealing a seething mass of what had once been entrails.

Baster hurriedly fitted the body together again and we covered it carefully with tins and newspaper, making a kind of little shed over it.

"She's the best one," he said, wiping his pencil on his coat sleeve and putting it into his pocket.

"Where d'you get her?" I asked.

"A chap sold it to me. His father drowned it," said Baster.

Our third and last discovery was the head of a large fish, hidden away in a corner of Baster's own backyard. It was even more offensive than the cat, and I refused to stay near the thing. I had begun to lose patience with Baster and his bodies.

"Now," he said, "I'll show you something special, only keep quiet," and he led the way into his house. We met no one in the kitchen and crept stealthily past the door leading to the shop, where, as Baster indicated with a jerk of his thumb, his father was working. Upstairs on all fours and into Baster's bedroom we slunk without a sound. He opened a low door that led to the roof space.

In here it was almost pitch dark and the smell of the warm air, that had been heated by the sun shining on the slates all day, was sickening. Again it was Baster's familiar smell. Only my curiosity kept me in the place. Presently Baster found a box of matches and struck one. We tiptoed our precarious way along the joists till we came to a place under the eaves, so low that we had to get on our hands and knees. Then the match went out and we were left in darkness. Baster struck another, and in the dim, flickering light I saw in front of me sheets of newspaper laid out on the lath and plaster between the beams. In the middle of each sheet lay a heap of little bones, some of them joined together with glue and wire and forming entire skeletons. There were skeletons of what looked like frogs and toads, of rats and mice, and a large one that seemed to be a rabbit's. Very carefully each bone, even the smallest, had been joined to the rest and fixed in its proper position. Other bones, some no bigger than a pin's head, lay in piles, not yet put together. Before the match was spent I noticed that one or two of them were not quite clean.

Baster asked me what I thought of them.

I replied, with truth, that I wished I had some skeletons.

Then he explained to me some of the difficulties of

skeleton collecting.

"It takes a long time," he whispered, as we sat on the floor in the dark. "The maggots take a long time to eat them up."

"Do you always wait till they've finished?" I asked him, thinking of what I had seen, and was then enduring.

No," he admitted.

"They smell, don't they?"

Baster did not answer. In the dark I could not tell whether he was offended at the suggestion.

"Another thing," he continued, "is the rats and the cats. They eat them and take them away."

"Doesn't your mother smell them?" I persisted.

"She thinks it's the drains," replied Baster, seriously.

Next day, while Screws was out of the classroom, I asked Baster a question that had been on my mind for some time. I asked it with a hesitation that stood in place of tact.

"You don't mind..." I began.

"What?"

"You don't mind being Stinker?"

"No," came the answer.

And, with more emphasis than I had ever known Baster to use: "Skeletons is more important."

* * *

Chapter 7

The Plymouth Brother

Mr. Egbert Primly sat in his shop, waiting for customers. All around him were stacked neat pyramids of oranges and lemons, and polished apples nesting in tissue paper cups. A delicious smell, proclaiming Spring, drifted in from the daffodils and hyacinths in the open window.

It was the Spring of 1917. In spite of what was going on over there, Spring came; the wonderful flowers poured out all their sweetness, were gathered, and found themselves in Mr. Primly's window. The demon War had not laid its red claw upon them, nor had it touched their owner. For the fruiterer was a Plymouth Brother and a Conscientious Objector.

Certainly Mr. Primly did not resemble a hero. In fact he looked, people said, every inch a Conscientious Objector. He was small and he was pale; his little red mouth curved like a woman's; you wondered whether his neck were really big enough to contain the necessary parts. His ladylike hands fidgeted nervously when they were not busy; when people spoke to him he cocked his head on one side and his mouth worked. And he had an irritating habit of perching himself on his toes and rocking backwards and forwards.

That he was a religious man was made plain to all comers by a text in letters made of twigs, which hung at the back of the shop:

> I WILL NEVER
> LEAVE THEE
> NOR FORSAKE THEE

One day, in a remote part of the town, he had been seen standing under a lamp-post preaching the Gospel to a crowd of children. One of them ended the meeting by letting off a squib just behind Mr. Primly. When the local tradesmen got to hear of it they understood vaguely why it was that Mr. Primly resisted all neighbourly overtures of friendship, refusing to discuss politics, matters of local importance, or indeed any topic of interest, and why Mrs. Primly hurried past the shopkeepers' wives in the street, with scarcely so much as a 'How are you keeping, Mrs. Jones?' or a 'And how's your little Tommy, Mrs. Smith?' Not that Mr. Primly rammed his religion down your throat — he was too meek a creature for that. He just avoided you and was quiet. Every one spoke of him as that queer little man.

Then the War came and Mr. Primly had to appear before a Tribunal. He told them, with a slightly surprising firmness, that he would not fight, because he was a Christian. One of the Tribunal, who was a retired army major, said that he had another name for a man who was too frightened to prevent bloodthirsty Huns butchering his wife and child. Primly just trembled and was silent. Finally they exempted him on grounds of National Importance. Since that occasion the townspeople's distrust had turned to hostility. Men whose sons were at the Front cursed Primly in the street and most of the neighbours cut him dead. Twice the shop window was smashed under mysterious circumstances. And women stood in their backyards thanking the Almighty, in voices raised for Mrs. Primly's benefit that their husbands were not shivering cowards, even if they did take a glass of beer sometimes and swear, and they didn't deserve to be shot, like the husbands of some women they knew.

In spite of all this Mr. Primly's business did not decline. Prices rose steadily, and, though the fruiterer's opinions were what they were, his potatoes and apples were beyond reproach, and such things were not everywhere to be had. His evident prosperity made the townsfolk even more angry. It was clear, they said, why Primly would not fight. He was coining money, as well as saving his wretched little skin. He was profiteering while their brave sons and husbands rotted and bled in Flanders mud, and, to cap it all, he was doing it under the cloak of religion — the wily shirker! From local pulpits, Mr. Primly was more than once denounced, in thinly veiled terms, as a Pharisee and a Judas.

All this appeared to affect the mild little shopkeeper not at all. He went on serving you quietly and politely, with perhaps a trifling remark about the weather and always a good down-scale. For twelve hours a day he worked, polishing his window, carting sacks of potatoes from the railway depot, dusting the counter, making wreaths of arum lilies and maiden-hair fern for the dead. Some mourners preferred these works of Mr. Primly's dainty fingers; others thought their money more wisely invested in those wondrous creations of convoluted tin leaves and wax lilies writhing under glass domes that adorned the walls of the shop. Mr. Primly had a fastidious eye and a nimble hand, and used to paint inscriptions to order on the porcelain tablets which rested in the midst of the floral ironmongery. Just now, one lay on the counter beside him. It had the shape of a heart, and the lettering was ornate and embroidered with fantastic flourishes. It ran:

> TO OUR DARLING
> SUE
> from her sorrowing
> MUM, DAD & UNCLE
> HERBERT
> "Safe in the arms
> of Jesus."

Mr. Primly gazed upon this memorial mournfully, wondering whether the epilogue were really true. Was Sue really safe in the arms of Jesus? Fervently he hoped so. Was the little girl saved, and did she now walk in heavenly mansions? That the pious footnote was by no means an assurance that Sue's mother and father had brought her up in the fear of the Lord, he knew well. For had he not once written on just such another porcelain heart the words: 'Come unto me all ye that labour, and I will give you rest,' at the request of a notorious drunkard who had hounded his wife to death? Only when Death the preacher speaks to these people, Mr. Primly reflected, does the light begin to shine feebly in their hearts, harder almost than porcelain. Ah that now, in these last terrible days, he might kindle many bright torches for God!

Another specimen of Mr. Primly's handicraft was affixed to the door of the shop. It was a small notice board, bearing, in gold letters on a dark background, the words:

> **MEETINGS**
> LORD'S DAY 11 A.M.
> &
> THE GOSPEL 7 P.M.
> All Welcome

On this Saturday afternoon, Mr. Primly sat behind the counter, wondering about little Sue and waiting for customers. They had been coming in all the morning, thick and fast. After lunch there came a welcome opportunity to put things in their places, restore the denuded pyramids of apples, bring in a fresh bag of potatoes from the shed at the back, sprinkle the floor with a watering can and sweep up the dust, and at last to rest for a minute or two. A broad beam of sunshine slanted across the shop and alighted on a tray of monkey nuts, resting on the counter. Along the narrow desolate street an army lorry jogged, and a dog began barking. Mr. Primly's head nodded.

Then came voices and hurrying footsteps, and two men passed the window and walked in. One of them was a tall fellow, well past middle age, with a ponderous red face and a yellow bristling moustache. His companion, a younger man, wore a butterfly collar and a bow tie. At once Mr. Primly roused himself and stood up.

"What can I get you sir?" he asked, inclining his head.

"Nothing," replied the elder of the two men, "nothing at all."

A pause followed, while he glanced around the shop.

"Doing nicely here, aren't you?"

The tone of his voice was harsh. Mr. Primly shuffled behind the counter.

"Fairly well, thank you," he faltered.

"How nice!" said the smaller man, smiling unpleasantly.

Another and longer pause, then,

"Mr. Primly, we want you to answer a question." He looked at his companion, who continued:

"What would you do if a German soldier walked in here just now and started sticking your baby like a pig?"

"I should pray, Mr. Carter," answered the shaking fruiterer.

Carter swore an oath that made Primly wince, and cried, "Supposing you had a rifle and were man enough to hold it, what then?"

"I should pray to the Lord."

Carter groaned, and started to pace the shop, kicking at the boxes and piles of vegetables. Then he walked towards Primly and, resting his hands on the counter, leaned forward and looked down on the upturned face of the fruiterer.

"Do you happen to remember my son, Mr. Primly?" he asked, very quietly. Primly, fascinated by his stare, gave what was apparently a nod of assent.

"Fine up-standing lad, wasn't he? Good looking too. He was going to make his mark in the world, wasn't he? Just turned twenty, six foot tall, and earning as much as his dad, wasn't he?"

Primly said nothing. Carter brought his face nearer and shouted, "Say something, you bleeding fool!"

"Yes," said Primly.

"Ah," broke in Green, the smaller man, imitating Primly's voice, "But he was a wicked sinner, wasn't he? Not a holy little man, hey?"

"Say something!" roared Carter at the shrinking Primly, whose face was twitching all over. Then, in almost a whisper, "His mother and I were fond of him, you know... Well, he was heathen enough to join up. We had news of him this morning. One of his legs, Mr. Primly, has been blown off, well above the knee. A stump left, that's all; a bleeding stump. How's that, Mr. Primly? And his face was scratched—just a matter of a cheek missing and all his teeth showing at one side."

"Oh it's all right," continued Green, "he's alive all right, don't worry. We thought you'd like to know."

Primly drew the back of his hand across his forehead, which was wet.

"Drop in and see him one day, he'd be delighted to see you. Specially as he got a face like that while he was fighting to get you your fat profits. Oh, he'll love to see you!"

"I'm sorry," moaned Primly, backing up against the wall fixture.

"Quite a nice friendly visit, Mr. Primly!" said Green, and walked towards the door. Then he turned round. "But we've forgotten something. Give me a pound of apples."

Primly came from behind the counter and bent over a tray of fruit. As he did so, Green grabbed him from behind and dragged him to the middle of the floor.

"Take that... and that... and that, " shouted Carter, hitting out at Primly's face with all his might, then pushing him forward. As he fell his head hit the edge of a shelf, and he lay amid the scattered fruits and vegetables, motionless, with the whites of his eyes showing above the pupils and a streak of blood at the corner of his mouth. For a moment the men stood looking at him. Then Mrs. Primly came in through the door at the back of the shop and, seeing her husband, gave a little cry. Green gave the prostrate body a kick, joined his friend in the doorway, and they walked away.

II

A few doors away from Mr. Primly's shop there was a new cinema, with a strong basement. The manager of this establishment had invited his neighbours to use this basement as a retreat during air raids. He had suggested to Mr. Primly that he and his family should shelter there, but Primly had replied, "The Lord will take care of us." The manager, who was a kindly man, shrugged his shoulders and left it at that.

At half past ten on Sunday morning a droning noise brought the people of Y... to their windows. They saw, high in the cloudless sky, four black shapes, like ravens bringing doom. Already around them puffs of white smoke grew suddenly from nothing. Then came reports, not like thunder crashes, but as if the ground were rending asunder, and echoes that might have been the death rattles of the earth itself. Above the drone a woman's voice wailed, in mortal terror...

In the cellar of the cinema a flickering oil lamp shown on a dozen faces, silhouetted against the darkness. The men, standing in a group to one side, were silent. Nobody took any notice of a small boy who, insensible of his danger, kept whining, "What's the matter, mother?" As if to answer him there came an ear-splitting crash, shaking the foundations of the building. A sudden and violent draught almost extinguished the lamp. An old woman, with grey hair falling over her face, sank in the corner and began alternately to pray and curse in a voice that was half a shriek. George Carter found himself clenching his hands so tightly that the nails almost punctured the skin of his palms, and a young woman with a baby in her arms was horribly sick where she stood...

A few doors down the street a little company was gathered in an upper room, which had been arranged as a place of worship, with chairs round the walls and a table in the middle. On the table was a white cloth, and on the cloth a flask of wine, a glass, and a basket holding a broken loaf. On one of the chairs sat Mrs. Primly in a black hat and gown, her face untroubled and her eyes quiet. In her left hand rested the hand of her daughter, a girl of seven years. On her right sat the young woman who served in the house.

In front of the table stood Egbert Primly, with one hand resting upon it. In the other hand he held a book, from which he was reading. His face, though it bore the marks of yesterday, was utterly transfigured. It shone. His whole frame had the dignity of a man, or more than a man, the serenity of one who is strong,—to the death, if need be.

He read:

"Behold, I stand at the door, and knock: if any man hear my voice and open the door, I will come in to him, and will sup with him, and he with me.

To him that overcometh will I grant to sit with me in my throne, even as I also overcame, and am set down with my Father in his throne."

Mrs. Primly raised her eyes and looked at her husband's face. It seemed to her at that moment, while the drone and roar of death went on without, that already Egbert Primly had overcome.

* * *

Chapter 8

Gerald's Thunderbolt

On the outskirts of a small provincial town on the coast of East Anglia there stood a weather-beaten roomy old house with two wings, enclosing a square paved courtyard. The upper floor of one of the wings consisted of a single low room known as the lumber room. One day, Gerald shifted all its legitimate contents, comprising sugar boxes loaded with useless books, great bundles of mouldy linen, a broken brass and iron bedstead and a mattress, to the far end of the room, leaving a clear space which he regarded as his own. Then over the door appeared a notice:

> MUSEUM
> admision 1d.
> Proffesor Gerald Hopperley F.K.S.
> CURATER

Around the walls of the museum were arranged the collections, all neatly displayed and catalogued. First there was a big but dilapidated showcase, the gift of a sympathetic tradesman, that contained rows of butterflies, all beautifully pinned out and ticketed. Gerald had, with infinite patience, bored many small holes in the bottom of the case and plugged them with cork to receive the pins, and covered them over with a sheet of clean paper. Each pin bore, in addition to the butterfly, a label on which were inscribed the creature's name in English and Latin, the place and date of its capture, and its sex, whether real or supposed. There were common Cabbage butterflies, exquisite Orange Tips, whose wings seemed to have fiery fingerprints on them, Ringlets as sooty as sweeps with little eye-spots underneath, Small Coppers whose wings might have been clipped out of a sheet of red metal, delicately veined Brimstones, Peacocks dusky and brilliant like Spanish beauties, and, best of all, a row of Holly Blues, whose trim little wings were powdered with forget-me-not coloured scales.

On the left of the butterflies stood a tray, lined with cotton-wool, upon which reposed a collection of birds' eggs, all labelled like the butterflies. A hoard of coins, scattered on the shelves of an old bookcase, stood on the left. These exhibits were, according to Gerald, more in the nature of make-weights or sops for the unscientific, calculated to attract the dull-witted type of visitor, than serious departments of the museum. The birds' eggs he had obtained from a country friend of his, in exchange for pilfered pastries and glass alleys. The coins had been bequeathed by his father. They were, he felt, altogether unworthy to be grouped with natural specimens—nasty, artificial things. Gerald heartily despised all collectors of stamps and coins and cigarette cards, heapers-up of man-made trash, and was really ashamed of his coins. "But there," he said, "when you have a museum the more you have to show the better, and the more people come."

An assortment of sea shells and another of fossils completed the exhibition. The shells were dusty and despised remnants of an outgrown enthusiasm, but the fossils were the show-piece of the museum. Many laborious afternoons spent poking clay boulders and searching shingle banks had yielded, in driblets of from two to twenty, several hundred specimens. Gerald set out on these occasions alone, armed with a stick and a bag, and trudged for miles along the beach till he came to a weird and fearsome place where stood grim blue cliffs. At their feet were piled huge masses of concrete, fallen walls, great derelict bastions and twisted bars of iron, all tumbled by wild seas that eddied and moaned, scooping out hollows and stirring treacherous quicksands. The footprints of rats—surely as big as rabbits—were always to be seen in the wet sand, and sometimes the horribly bloated carcase of a drowned dog lay festering in drifts of seaweed. Here if anywhere in the world, Gerald believed, the octopus and the giant squid lay in wait, and fleshy sea-anemones covered with clay-slime fed all the while on sailors' bodies washed up by the tide. Only once did Gerald see a human being there—a very fierce old man sitting in a cave, muttering and drawing pictures in the sand.

The boulder clay of the cliffs contained great numbers of fossils, but few kinds. Nearly all of Gerald's specimens were either ammonites or belemnites. The ammonites were flat spiral shells made of solid stone—hundreds of them, of all shapes and sizes, resting on long strips of cotton-wool. Some had been polished by the sea till they were almost irrecognisable, others were serrated with precise patterns, and one, in particular, had a beautiful coat of mother of pearl that shone with many colours. Gerald had discovered their name from a book about geology and had even tried to sort them into distinct varieties, but Gerald's uncle persistently referred to them as 'petrified snakes'. In vain did Gerald protest, pointing out that for all of them to have lost their heads was a curious coincidence, and demanding to know why each one had died in such a neatly curled attitude. Neither the evidence of the geological treatise nor Gerald's often repeated objections to the snake theory could shake the belief of his guardian, and Aunt Amelia was constrained to send her nephew early to bed for daring to contradict his elders. From time to time Gerald wrote a label, "*Ammonites*, thought by the ignorant to be petrified snakes," and placed it at the top of the exhibition, and as often Aunt Amelia removed it, rebuking Gerald by word and deed.

But the belemnites—objects resembling nothing so much as sharp-nosed bullets of stone—were the source of a more bitter contention. Uncle Edward, looking kindly upon Gerald's researches, discovered among his possessions a certain priceless object and presented it, with some parade of self-sacrifice, to Gerald. This treasure was, according to Uncle Edward, a thunderbolt, and it had been discovered by him upon a gravel path in the town of Saxmundham after a most violent thunderstorm. For years he had preserved it in a little wooden box, but upon the foundation of the museum he felt that the boy's thirst for knowledge should be stimulated by a gift. This good deed was wasted upon Gerald, who irreverently suggested that a thunderbolt was really as it were a ball of electricity, about the size of a cricket ball but extraordinarily difficult to handle. He insinuated that Uncle Edward was not the sort of man that coolly carried a thunderbolt in his trouser pocket—Gerald called to mind magnificent biblical persons who held lightnings in their hands, but the role seemed unsuited to the fat little store keeper. The upshot of the conversation was that Gerald was confined to his bedroom until he would confess the true nature of the object. After three days of solitary confinement he was released at the instance of Aunt Amelia, with a caution, but without having subscribed to the thunderbolt theory. Thereafter the thing lay on the table among the other belemnites, and over them all appeared the notice:

"*Belemnites*, supposed by the very superstitious to be thunderbolts."

Since Uncle Edward, however, was a strong-minded man, subject to fits of violence, the label was invariably missing when he was near.

During the holidays Gerald spent the greater part of his waking life in the museum, deriving untold satisfaction from the brilliance of his butterflies, the perfection and antiquity of his fossils, and above all from the consciousness of his sole ownership of both. The hub of his uncle's world was the draper's shop in the High Street which he managed, and its circumference was the town's politics, which he would have liked to manage. The totality of Aunt Amelia's existence embraced, so far as Gerald was aware, nothing of more transcendent importance than the current price of best surloin of beef and the brilliance of her brass door-knobs. So Gerald was left to his own devices, reading a great deal, and seriously, for his age and roaming all over the nearer country till he knew every dyke on the marshes and every breakwater along the shore for miles around. The more he saw and read the less he respected his guardians. They never wearied of reminding him that he was young and therefore ignorant and that they were old and wise, and Gerald never wearied of gathering knowledge, as much to prove his uncle a fool as for its own sake. And Gerald became sure that his collections were of the utmost scientific value, and almost believed that he was a venerable 'professor' in charge of an extension of the British Museum. He would much rather have lost his right eye than his best Brimstone butterfly or the pearly ammonite. On one occasion his uncle threatened to confiscate the collection, and it was at once plain that here lay Gerald's one vulnerable spot.

Gerald boasted that his fossils were "millions and millions and millions of years old."

"Nonsense," said his uncle, "They're antediluvian shells, that's what they are. And they can't be even six thousand years old because the world was created in 4004 B.C." He got out his bible and showed Gerald the date printed in the margin, next to the first chapter of Genesis.

"It's a lie," replied Gerald, uncompromisingly.

Then came the awful threat of confiscation, which at once subdued Gerald.

"All right then," he said, "they're antediluvian shells, that's all." In view of this admission Uncle Edward merely boxed his ears and sent him upstairs as punishment for insolence.

That evening, as Gerald sat in the museum trying to read a book about the Mesozoic monsters, the sky darkened and big raindrops began to fall. He went to the window and looked out. Clouds like lumps of clay were blowing over from the sea and piling up so that they filled the sky. A three-forked lightning flash, shooting up into the clouds, astonished Gerald by its likeness to Jack's beanstalk of flame, flourishing and fading instantly. He counted the seconds: one... two... three... four... five... six... then came the great crackling roar, subsiding gradually into muffled booms that echoed away and away among cliffs and bastions of cloud, losing themselves in the far distance. Between the lace curtains of the window opposite Gerald could see a fire burning and the figure of Uncle Edward — paunchy, absurd little man, with a newspaper resting on his knees — thrown up in relief. His bald pate, his pince-nez and the tips of his waxed moustaches, edged with orange light, were just visible through the streaming window. Faster and faster the rain came down till Uncle Edward was no more than a hateful dark blur, seen through a cataract of water. The rain in the gutters overflowed and poured in rivers down the walls, filling the courtyard with a lake of hissing water...

Gerald wondered whether Uncle Edward would pick up any thunderbolts after this storm...

Two minutes later there was a tremendous thunderclap and a blinding flash, followed instantly by the sound of smashing glass and a shriek.

* * *

Now Gerald's acquaintances are charged 2d for admission to the museum, which contains, as the notice on the door says, "a special new attraction."

The attraction has a little glass case all to itself, presented by Uncle Edward and Aunt Amelia. Inside the case, resting on a bed of wadding, lies a pointed stony object, broken into three pieces. The superscription, in Gerald's handwriting, reads thus:

THUNDERBOLT

which struck this house and wounded

EDWARD AUGUSTUS HOPPERLEY ESQUIRE

in the leg

3rd September 1935 A.D.

So far, Gerald has collected 2/8 in admission fees, and, because he has assured his uncle of his sincere conversion to the thunderbolt theory, he has been granted 1/- a week pocket money.

As a precautionary measure he has buried his catapult in the garden.

* * *

Chapter 9

Miss Clarissa

Miss Clarissa was a wonderful woman. She liked everybody and trusted everybody. The very cats that rooted up her bulbs and raspberry canes were misled cats rather than bad cats. The tradesmen, of course, took advantage of Miss Clarissa's simplicity, gave her short change and shorter weight, and cooked the monthly accounts, when first she came to the town. Then, for some reason not clearly known to themselves, they would begin doing little things for her 'just to oblige' and presently she found that housekeeping was not nearly so expensive.

The man who sold her the little house where she lived, in one of the town's shabbiest back streets, made a lot of money out of the transaction. But then, a few months after, he went to her and said that he had a stove and some lengths of shelving that he didn't want, and there were a couple of his men idle that he wanted to keep on, and might he do a thing or two about the house? When Miss Clarissa told her friends about these benefactions they wouldn't believe her — why, the man was the biggest twister in the whole town! But there they were, the smart new stove, the beautiful shelves in the cupboard, and the front parlour bright and gay, reeking of new paint and distemper. And Miss Clarissa not a penny the worse for it all!

When she took the cottage in the shabby back street she was about forty-five years old, with white woolly hair and a big face without the suspicion of a wrinkle. A fresh and a young face it was, not pretty, but in a fashion handsome; you felt that her eyes had never rested on anything evil. When she talked, no matter to whom, her face lighted up with pleasure, and she never had anything sorrowful to say. At least, coming from her, such sorrowfulness as there was in it seemed transmuted.

Of course she had her little faults and weaknesses, though these suited her and seemed quite proper. For instance, she talked a great deal, she talked to everybody, and she talked about her own experiences. But they were remarkable experiences, really worth talking about. Things happened to Miss Clarissa, exciting things and providential; her life was an Odyssey and there was nothing mundane in it at all. The cat that grubbed up her crocuses was an astonishing cat, of a curious manner of life, a feline mystery. As for the crocuses—if you couldn't see how wonderful a thing a crocus is, the world might as well be a rubbish dump as far as you were concerned! But even if it had been a rubbish dump Miss Clarissa would have found all sorts of treasures in it. No doubt but what she romanced now and then about her experiences. But then she was a romantic lady. She had a gift to see the world differently from ordinary people.

Miss Clarissa's family—her brother Herbert and her brother Oliver—resembled her. Herbert had been a clever engineer and the manager of a big factory, then one day he took it into his head to leave the factory and his comfortable home and go preaching. With no more than his clothes on his back and his bible in his pocket, he went off to the Shetland Isles. He walked all over the islands, having wonderful deliverances from snow-drifts and storms and perils of all kinds, and used to call at every house he came to, reading his bible to the people and telling them about the love of God. The fishermen and the crofters would give the white-haired gentleman porridge and shelter and listen to him attentively. Mr Herbert thought it was the love of God working in them. It is probable that if he had preached the love of anything else they would have given him porridge and shelter just the same. People who met him never forgot him. He was very tall and gentle voiced, he talked in a kind of hurried, high-pitched whisper, and his face always bore a look of exaltation.

At quite an early age Oliver, the other brother, had given up his practice in London—he was a physician—and gone to a leper island, off the east coast of Canada, where he remained till he died, looking after the lepers.

One day Miss Clarissa suddenly determined to go and see her

brother Oliver, on his leper island. With scarcely any preparation for the journey she got on a liner and sailed to Canada. There she found that the boat which carried supplies to the island sailed only once a month, and there were three weeks to go till the next sailing. So she found a man with a little motor boat who promised to take her across. When they were half way a violent storm arose, the boat shipped a lot of water, and, to make matters worse, the engine stopped. The boatman, who could only speak French, and was trembling with terror, began to curse Miss Clarissa for having tempted him out of port on such a night. But she knelt down in the water at the bottom of the boat and said a prayer. After that the storm subsided a little and she began baling out the water with her hat. They improvised some oars, and after many hours of rowing and baling they reached Leper Island. Only his exhausted condition prevented the boatman from worshipping Miss Clarissa as a saint. He didn't even ask for more money.

She stayed and helped Oliver for a month or two, during which time she saved her niece from drowning, built a shed, dug a well and nearly buried herself in it, helped to install a telephone so that she would be able to talk to the lepers (she was not allowed to go near them, of course), and had many other peculiar experiences.

Then she went to China, with a vague intention of doing some missionary work. As soon as she got there she boarded a Chinese vessel bound for the interior, and sailed far up the Yangtze Kiang. Sure enough she was the only white woman on the boat, and sure enough they were attacked by bandits and made prisoners. That was how she learned Chinese cooking and a little of the Chinese language. The bandits never got any ransom for her and after a while they ceased to bother about it. Miss Clarissa nursed the men when they were sick, cooked their meals, and made herself generally useful. She always described the bandit chief as 'a dear man, really,' and was sure that she had converted him from his banditry.

Other marvels happened to Miss Clarissa after she came back to England. But at last, when she was forty five, she thought she would like a little house of her own, with a bit of a garden to dig in and a cheerful fire to sit by in the evening, when she would remember all that had happened. So she bought the cottage in the mean back street in Beccles and settled down, as she firmly believed, for the rest of her life. But within three months she was restive and within a year she was gone to find her brother Herbert, who, she thought, had lost himself somewhere in Bechuanaland. As a matter of fact he had gone somewhere else to find Miss Clarissa.

While she lived in Beccles, Miss Clarissa used to take long walks into the country. Striding along, clad in a long dark skirt and a silk blouse covered with little red flowers, and with heavy boots on her feet, she would cover many miles of country in an afternoon. Her beautiful white head of hair, done up into a bun behind, used to go bobbing along the lanes, and when it reflected the sun it could be seen for miles, shining like a beacon. She made many friends upon these journeys. She talked to tramps and poachers, played with children, watched the birds and the cattle, got rebuked for trespassing but always ended on the most friendly terms with the party trespassed against, fell into ditches and extricated herself, and heard the queerest tales. And everyone she met was pleasant to her, charmed by her gentle, half-timorous manner and her smiling face.

A favourite walk of hers was by the marshes that lay near the town. Here was a kind of low cliff, partly covered with thin dry grass and furze bushes, that commanded a magnificent view of the marsh-lands. On this bank she used to look for harebells, and rest before going home.

One afternoon late in May, Miss Clarissa sat on the grass near the top of the bank, just out of the wind and just in the sun, which was as warm as if it had been August. The delicious scent of the furze below drifted up to where she was, mingling with the all-pervading smell of the marshes. Small white clouds like snowballs hung over the marshes and high in the blue sky a heron flew, with its enormous neck outstretched, uttering its doleful cry. Miss Clarissa watched it till it was a dot, lost in the far fringe of trees that bounded the marshes on the south.

For miles and miles, as far as she could see, the marsh-lands stretched to the west, utterly flat, like a luscious green tablecloth, without a hedge or a tree or a farmhouse, and not so much as a man in sight. All the year round the grass was green, nourished by the dykes that never dried up. Straight canals of dark stagnant water were these dykes, that encircled every patch of grass. For the most part they were covered with a green scum of duck-weed, but even where the water was visible it looked turbid and you couldn't see three inches below the surface. Shiny black whirligigs disported themselves endlessly on the water, describing innumerable circles like skaters. There were less pleasant creatures there too — water scorpions with their great blood-sucking jaws like pincers, and malevolent slimy things. Miss Clarissa, whose insatiable interest in all living things atoned for her ignorance of them, cherished a hidden belief that the unfathomable mud at the bottom of the dykes was infested with alligators. She had, in fact, seen the nose of one of them sticking up out of the water. It had plunged below when she approached.

The marshes were, she believed, nothing but a sea of mud, overlaid with a skin of turf. A farmer had once told her about a cow that had disappeared before his very eyes, had sunk down and down into the marsh mud till only the tips of its horns were visible. And the odd thing about it was that the turf had been there, complete and undisturbed, over the spot where the cow had gone down!

Miss Clarissa remembered how frightened she had been one day when, as she was walking along the cart track just below the bank where she sat now, she had heard a loud whinnying sound, as though at her side. She looked all round, but there was not a horse in sight. The nearer marshes were quite empty. A quarter of a mile away some cows were grazing — nothing else. She had come to the conclusion that she had witnessed a kind of auditory mirage when the whinnying started again, not a yard from her. It was a loud and distressed cry and it appeared to come from the dyke on her right. Treading carefully on the treacherous earth, she went as near to the water's edge as she dared. What she saw nearly made her fall in with astonishment. A horse's head, a live horse's head, sticking up out of the duckweed, as though it were floating there! Miss Clarissa began to wonder whether there were really such a thing as a water horse, when the head started to rear, revealing the poor creature's shoulders all covered with gleaming scum. It began to neigh and white foam gathered on its lips.

As soon as the truth dawned upon her, Miss Clarissa ran as fast as her legs could carry her to the farmhouse half a mile beyond the cliff bank, having first marked the spot by means of a handkerchief with a stone on it to keep it from blowing away. She found the farmer leaning over his gate and told him about the horse's head. Off he ran and fetched a thick rope and a whip, hopped on his bicycle and rode away, with Miss Clarissa perched precariously on the step. On the way they summoned two labourers, who trotted behind, vainly attempting to hide their amusement at the pair on the bicycle.

When at last they had got the rope round the hind quarters of the horse, Miss Clarissa insisted upon helping them to pull it out. It was a terribly difficult job, but she was spurred on by the thought of alligators attacking the poor horse's legs. At the end, when the horse had been safely landed, Miss Clarissa was drenched with water and daubed with mud. She spent the evening at the farmer's house, arrayed in his dressing gown, while her clothes hung steaming on a clothes-horse in front of the fire. Things like that were always happening to Miss Clarissa when she went walking.

But today, as yet, nothing noteworthy had happened to her, and she was rather glad. It was so peaceful sitting there in the warm sun, with the earth spread out below. She felt comfortable and drowsy.

Miss Clarissa was a little surprised when two red blurs began to form against the background of the grass, some distance away. A most extraordinary bright red they were, though she could see the grass and a cow behind them, or rather, through them. The blurs grew more and more luminous and their edges more and more distinct. Horrors! They were actually a pair of red demons, hand in hand. They had wide demon mouths with loathsome, demoniacally gleeful grins, and bright little demon eyes. They looked at Miss Clarissa; clearly they saw her. She looked away hurriedly, pretending not to have noticed them, but wherever she looked, there they were, glowing like tongues of flame, and grinning. Then, still holding hands, they began to dance, if you could call such antics dancing. Their legs — thin little red stalks with feet like buds — capered this way and that, bending monstrously at the knees, becoming amazingly elongated, then stumpy, and all the while keeping perfect time. Faster and faster the legs danced with such incredible agility that she could not follow them, but the bodies did not dance. They remained absolutely still, as though the writhing red stalks below didn't belong to them, and the faces bore the same wickedly merry smile. Miss Clarissa felt very apprehensive, but she couldn't help being a little amused at their funny dance. They didn't come nearer. She knew they were biding their time.

Stealthily Miss Clarissa crept behind a huge rock, snatched up a heavy stone, and waited.

Presently came footsteps, a little pitter patter on the cart track below, and she braced herself for the fight.

But there was no fight because the author of the footsteps began to whistle the tune of Michael Finnagin, and then to sing the words about Michael Finnagin's whiskers, in a small voice, very much out of tune. Obviously no demon, Miss Clarissa thought.

So she dropped her handbag and peeped round the gorse bush. It was only a little boy. Such a charming little boy too, she observed.

He had fair curling hair and blue eyes and though his clothes were untidy and worn he was a clean, bright little boy. He stopped and inspected everything, loitering, sitting down and running about like a small dog. He threw handfuls of dirt in the dyke, kicked stones, whistled and sang, chased a butterfly, and finally sat down just opposite Miss Clarissa. Miss Clarissa was very fond of small boys, though she was a little afraid of them sometimes. But this one was a pleasant little fellow; the back of his head was so nice that she felt quite sentimental about it. Should she climb down the bank and give him tuppence?

Then something caught the little boy's eye; Miss Clarissa could not see what it was. He got up ran forward a few paces, and picked up a small object that struggled in his hands. He looked at it for a moment and put it in his pocket. After that he seemed uncertain what to do.

Presently an idea seemed to come into his head. He went to the edge of the dyke and plucked a thin reed. Then he snipped off a length and blew through it, apparently making sure that there were no obstructions. Having sat down again, he put the reed in his mouth and took the creature—surely it was a frog—from his pocket, holding it by the hind legs.

Miss Clarissa leaned forward, peering through the gorse bushes. She was curious, for she couldn't believe that the small boy would be unkind to the frog, or whatever it was.

With a gasp of horror she saw him push the reed into the frog and blow. He blew and blew, till the frog swelled out like a balloon.

As she rushed down the bank the frog burst, making a horrible mess. When the boy saw her he took to his heels and raced along the cart track, while Miss Clarissa gave chase.

As she ran the tears fell like rain on the flowers that covered her blouse, blinding her eyes so that she nearly fell into the dyke. On and on she ran till there was no breath left in her body and her heart felt as though it would burst. The boy had run out of sight, and lay hidden among the gorse bushes. Slowly Miss Clarissa walked back to the place where she had been sitting.

When she had done weeping she said a prayer for the boy and the frog and rested herself, then she went home.

The next day she wrote a letter to her brother Herbert about an astonishing, awful dream that she had dreamed while resting on the bank overlooking the marsh-lands, a dream about demons and a little boy. But to her friends that day she seemed wistful, even a little sad—an uncommon thing in Miss Clarissa.

* * *

Chapter 10

St. Sebastian

Gerald lay on the couch beside the window. He was wearing his night-shirt and his dressing-gown, and a pink eider-down quilt was wrapped round him from the waist downwards. His back was propped up on a number of cushions, so that he was half sitting, half reclining.

It was about the time of his eleventh birthday, and he was recovering from an operation for appendicitis.

From where he lay, Gerald could look out of the window into the garden, and a lovely sight it was. The sun shone bright and warm for early April, with that glow which is doubly welcome after a harsh winter and months of murky, bitter weather. Two almond trees in full bloom stood on either side of the lawn, quite near the window, and the borders were full of half-hidden violets, moist, voluptuous hyacinths, velvet primulas and hosts of daffodils. Gerald could look up at the sky through the black boughs of the nearer almond tree, whose pink flowers made the blue of the sky seem a thousand times deeper and nearer, and incredibly bright. The delicate blossom scarcely shook at all, so quiet was the morning, but occasionally a little shower of pink and white petals would loosen themselves from the tree and glide slowly down to the grass, and one or two would drift into the room and settle on the eider-down or on the carpet.

By Gerald's side there stood a low table with a bowl of mimosa, whose fluffy golden balls and delicious scent filled him with delight. The comfortable warmth of the sunlight, the scents and colours of the flowers, new-born and not yet dried after their bath of the morning dew, the broad expanse of sky without clouds, made him feel very cheerful. He did not mind being an invalid at all. In fact, he preferred convalescence to full health, with its attendant plague of school and a heap of troubles.

He never tired of lying on the couch all day, alone. There was so much to do. When he grew weary of observing the blackbirds and thrushes gadding about on the lawn, and the sparrows as they chased one another from the hedge to the almond trees and back again, he read such books as A Basket of Flowers and A Peep Behind the Scenes, or wrote Poetry, or painted, or just rested in a dreamy, happy state, looking up at the trees. And often he would think about all that had happened to him since the day he fell ill.

A little over six weeks ago he had been smitten with an agonising pain in his middle. Aunt Amelia had packed him off to bed immediately and dosed him with all her favourite nostrums — herbal teas, homoeopathic tinctures and any amount of castor oil and fig syrup. She read her Doctor's Book again and again, and treated Gerald for more complaints than anyone would have thought possible. But at the end of it all he was so much worse that Uncle Edward insisted that the doctor should be consulted in person.

So one evening the doctor had come to see Gerald. He was a burly man with a tooth-brush moustache, so tall that he narrowly avoided cracking his head on the beams over the bedroom, and he wore a greatcoat that reached down to his ankles, like a Russian soldier. Puffing a cloud of steam from his mouth, he strode up to the bed, ripped off the bed-clothes, hoisted Gerald's night-shirt and bellowed:

"Belly ache, what? Ha ha!"

Evidently he thought it was a great joke.

Then he made his knuckles into a sort of pick-hammer, with which he pounded Gerald's stomach all over. But Gerald was past caring.

That evening his aunt had wrapped him in blankets, his uncle had carried him downstairs into a cab that was waiting at the front door, and they had driven off to the hospital.

Only dimly did Gerald remember gazing at the white ceiling of the operating theatre and listening to the clatter of instruments, the hiss of boiling water, and the nurses talking in low tones, till one of them held over his face an object that reminded him of the hairy dome with which his aunt stuffed out the bun of her hair. He had a faint recollection of having counted up to twenty, or thereabouts, before the chloroform had put him to sleep.

After the first three or four days of sickness, coughing that hurt him terribly, and general discomfort, he began really to enjoy life in the men's ward. The wounded soldiers used to tell him marvellous stories of the war, after the lights had been put out for the night, and the nurses paid him a lot of attention because he was the 'baby' of the ward. Grandpa, the terrible old man who cursed all the while, spat at the nurses, and eventually died; the Catholic boy in the next bed who stuck his fingers in his ears throughout the ward service on Sunday; the ward gramaphone which played incessantly a song that sounded like:

> If by you and you, ou,
> If by you and you, ou-ou, ou-ou,

were all novel and entertaining.

But each morning had brought the ordeal of wound-dressing. Sometimes it was the matron, sometimes the burly doctor, who came round with a kind of dinner-waggon loaded with lint and hot water and fearsome tools. Kindly but firmly he, or she, would undo the bandages that swathed his middle, rip off the dressing whether it stuck or no, and examine and wash the wound. The wound reminded Gerald of a red centipede whose legs were the stitches and whose head was the blob at the top, where there was a little tube. Often the matron or the doctor would take a tool like a sacking needle and drive it inches into the centipede's head. Gerald always began to cry out when the point of the probe was about half an inch above the wound, and continued to complain till it was safely out again. He could scarcely feel the probe, of course; it was the look of the thing that appalled him. The Catholic boy was more strong-minded in this matter of probing. He used to grip the bars at the head of his bed, shut his eyes, and never open them again till the dressing was over. Gerald insisted upon supervising all that was done to him. He wanted to know the reason for everything and sometimes volunteered a suggestion.

One day the centipede's legs, that is to say the stitches, were cut with a pair of scissors, pulled out while Gerald lamented bitterly, and afterwards presented to him. They now lay in a matchbox on the table by his side. After the unstitching, the centipede's body had grown paler every day, but its head remained as red and as big as ever. The probing continued and sometimes the doctor daubed a white caustic substance upon the head, causing Gerald a sleepless night.

But the compensations had been ample, especially since he had come home again. Dorothy, the maid, would sometimes take him about in a bath-chair, wheeling him up the hill to the park to see how the crocuses were getting on, or, later, to look at the sprouting horse-chestnut trees. On these occasions Gerald used to chat with certain old gentlemen of his acquaintance who were out for their daily strolls, and instruct them in the mysteries of appendicitis, sketching diagrams for their enlightenment upon the rug wrapped round his knees. One old fellow stoutly maintained that he had no such thing as an appendix, and Gerald became quite heated. And when they said, politely, that they hoped that he would soon be up and about again, he shocked them by declaring that he intended to be ill until the summer holidays had begun. After that he would probably decide to get better again—probably, he had not made his mind up about it.

"Illness," he would whisper to them so that Dorothy should not overhear, "Illness is very nice: calves-foot jelly every morning at eleven, no school, and everyone treating you as though you was an angel!" He would exchange a wink and a laugh with the old chaps and on they would go.

But Gerald did not spend a great deal of time thinking about these events. He was a boy of deeds. First and foremost, he painted.

His box of colours, his brushes, saucers and water pot lay on the side table. Every day, for three hours and upwards, he painted. For subject he had one thing only, and that was St. Sebastian, who hung on the wall opposite the couch.

St. Sebastian was a man, nearly as large as life, printed on a roll of shiny canvas. He poised himself gracefully upon one leg while the other hung limp in the air; he held his arms away from his sides as though he were performing some physical exercise; he crooked and parted his fingers delicately as though he were playing upon an invisible piano. The expression on his face was one of saintly adoration, mingled with abysmal stupidity. And he was quite naked.

In all these particulars St. Sebastian showed no great oddity. The really remarkable thing about him, Gerald pointed out, was that he had, to all appearances, committed hara-kiri just before a flight of arrows had embedded themselves in his body. For all the way up St. Sebastian's middle there ran a great gash from which the flesh had receded, revealing to the world the whole of his interior; and every organ and artery and vein and muscle was set forth in detail and cunningly tinted and shaded. In each organ there was lodged an arrow, fearfully barbed, with a short description of the pierced organ in a little circle at the end where the feathers should have been. And in spite of all these torments St. Sebastian, like the true saint he was, showed not a trace of agitation or annoyance.

Mrs Bonigar, a middle-aged lady with a passion for illnesses, had lent St. Sebastian to Gerald so that he should understand where his appendix had been situated. She and Gerald had spent an interesting hour alone together, during which time she explained to him the nature of appendicitis, how it was caused by the growth, into a small plant, of a plumstone or other seed that had become mislaid inside the appendix. Gerald proved a willing pupil, asking innumerable questions, to all of which Mrs Bonigar supplied ingenious answers. He learnt that an operation for appendicitis is much like the mending of a puncture in a bicycle tyre: first your outer cover is removed, then some yards of your inner tube, as Mrs. Bonigar delicately termed Gerald's bowels, are hoicked out, patched up and stuffed back again. When it is all over you pack up your spanners and appendix patches and hope to goodness the patch holds. Gerald's, happily, was holding. She hoped it would continue to do so. Along with St. Sebastian she brought her own appendix, pickled in spirit, to show Gerald. She refused to let him keep it, however, least he should undo the stopper of the bottle and examine the appendix at closer quarters, but she agreed to leave the picture of the Saint.

St. Sebastian had been christened as such with the aid of Gerald's four-volume encyclopedia. Directly he read about the sufferings of the Saint he recognised the identity of the portrait, and the article upon Japan seemed to throw some light upon the condition of the Saint's middle. Then, a week after his return from the hospital, he decided that St. Sebastian deserved a more colourful, a more complicated, portrait. For three weeks Gerald had been working upon this portrait, adding improvements every day. Today, he was not sure what else he could put on the drawing.

It lay pinned to a small cooking-board, on the table. He picked it up and rested it against his knees, which were drawn up underneath the quilt. Certainly the painting seemed to have reached comple-tion. The Saint on the wall was a ghost, a wraith of a Sebastian with pale spectres of organs, a dim, spineless creature, when you compared him with the full-blooded, roaring Saint of Gerald's picture. Gerald had made him live, had made him very real, very horrible, a shocking and fascinating sight. Mrs Bonigar had been entranced with the painting and had demanded a copy, but he had not dared show it to his aunt for fear she should faint. Gerald was quite aware of its powerful qualities, for he had observed its effect upon Dorothy and the cat. Dorothy had screamed and next day she had complained of the nightmare. The cat had also behaved strangely. It was a remarkable painting.

Gerald had interpreted his subject freely, amending where amend-ments seemed called for, adding this and that as his fancy dictated. The original left one in doubt as to whether St. Sebastian were a man or a woman. Gerald's version removed this doubt. He was a man, decently furnished, as an afterthought, with a voluminous pair of violet pantaloons. Mrs Bonigar's Sebastian had pale, watery eyes, a little Greek nose, hairless womanly limbs, delicate fingers and not a single whisker. Gerald's had fierce green eyes in vermilion sockets, a great rhomboid nose, hefty mis-shapen limbs covered all over with hair like a hearth-rug, podgy fingers flashing with ruby rings, filthy nails, the curled beard of an Assyrian man-bull and mustachios whose limits were those of the paper itself.

These things had not been the work of a moment. Sudden inspirations, experiments with form and colour that lasted for hours, and excursions into books, had produced these improvements one by one. Gerald made it a rule to add something every day. When the straight-forward and obvious had been completed, then came the time for elaboration. St. Sebastian's teeth, for instance, were not plain dentures that you could have drawn and painted in an hour or so. They were fangs, barbed, serrated and polished, and each was of a unique pattern and colour. One was covered with a spiral ornament. Another had a deep hole in it, burrowed by an ill-natured dentist; and a nerve, shown as a little white baby screaming with pain, lay curled at its centre. The eye teeth were banded with bice green, and they curved like ram's horns so that they punctured small holes in St. Sebastian's cheek, from which two drops of blood ran down. Unlike a saint, Sebastian smoked a meerschaum, a corona-corona and a cigarette in a long silver holder. His hat was a grey trilby worn at a rakish angle and full of the moth. Gerald had depicted each moth-maggot with jaws like a shark's, working ravenously. One day, when he had been at a loss to know what to do next, he had made St. Sebastian into a sailor and tattooed his entire body, not excepting his lungs and kidneys and eyeballs, with patterns such as he had seen on seamen's arms. Twin hearts impaled on arrows, full-rigged schooners and all manner of sea craft, lovers' knots, serpents, griffins, mermaids and every kind of legendary beast, were scattered impartially over the whole of St. Sebastian' body and pantaloons.

If the outer Sebastian was curious and elaborate, his inner self was much more so. Every organ — hearts, lungs, stomach, liver, pancreas and all the rest — Gerald had drawn with scrupulous care. But, unable to restrain either his pencil or his brush, he had added many strange devices, some to serve as orthopaedic appliances, others merely on account of their decorative qualities. Thus he had supplied

St. Sebastian with an electric fan in either lung to assist respiration; with a complicated motor contrivance, which included an unorthodox steam-engine, to accelerate the beating of the heart; and a pump to ensure the proper movement of the bowels. For aesthetic reasons the heart had blushing cheeks, a pair of dimples and a hint at eyes and mouth, the stomach stood out bravely in royal blue, the lungs were cadmium yellow, the kidneys and liver alizarin crimson, the pancreas Hooker's green. There were no large areas of plain colour. What with the white and red blood corpuscles that infested every vein and artery, the loathsome tapeworms that writhed in the stomach and intestines, the convolutions, orthodox and imaginary, of every organ, and the supplementary machinery, every inch of St. Sebastian's surface had been fully utilized.

It had taken Gerald a fortnight to complete the body and another week to finish the background. The air about the Saint was thick with arrows, prodigiously mounted with peacock's feathers and screw head like gimlets, causing pitiful wounds that ran with ultramarine blood. At a later stage Gerald had filled in the remaining spaces — though the arrows were as thick as the seeds on a dandelion head — with viridian unicorns, satyrs, hobgoblins and a facsimile of Satan himself, winged, hoofed and scorpion-tailed, grasping a trident with which he appeared to be combing St. Sebastian's hair, and breathing terrible blasphemies into the Saint's ear. And ranged round Satan were the four Virtues and the four Sins.

The first virtue was Work, a wizened boy-beast, creased with innumerable wrinkles and quite bald except for a fringe of snow-white hair. His enormous pink brain was full to overflowing with little grey surds, isobars, hypotenuses and gerunds, all carefully drawn with the aid of Gerald's magnifying glass. Sport was the second virtue. His nose had been flattened into a mushroom in the course of many boxing bouts; his biceps stood out like wens; his body was as hairy as a woman's head; and his brain, a vermilion full stop, was all but invisible. Goodness, the angel-boy, had a daisy chain hanging round his neck and the Holy Trinity seated inside his brain-pan.

The fourth, Cleanliness, was an infant in Chinese white, with gross features and odious brilliantined hair, sitting in a bath-tub. For brain he had a sponge.

Relatively, the four Sins were well-favoured. Falsehood, a Janus-faced child, was prettily coloured but not otherwise remarkable. Cribbing, the chameleon-eyed, contemplated with his left eye a shirt cuff and finer nails that were chock-a-block with illegal information in infinitesimal handwriting, while his right was solemnly glued to an examination paper. A beautiful lady in corsets, copied straight from Aunt Amelia's fashion journal, was anonymous, and seemed to occupy a position intermediate between the Virtues and the Sins. And an unspeakably handsome little boy with jet black hair, caught in the act of setting light to a school-master's trousers with a stick of phosphorous, had the title General Mischief written under him, and was none other than Gerald himself.

Yesterday, Gerald had done a rash deed. He had filled such intervening spaces as remained in the background, with black paint. This had thrown up into high relief all the creatures on the picture, including the Saint, and had notably improved the whole effect. But it had also prevented further additions. Gerald feared that the painting was finished at last. There was nothing else to do now but admire it all.

This Gerald did without stint. He contemplated every detail till he knew it by heart. Especially he liked those portions of the picture which had been conceived and executed when his temperature had been somewhat above the normal. The tapeworms, for example, both surprised and delighted him. The products of an earlier, a more feverish imagination, they baffled him, he could not remember having painted any of them. It was as though they had been drawn, when he had been asleep one night, by some crazy goblin hand. Beautiful and wicked they were, with heads that, if you squinted and looked slant-wise at them, resembled the features of Uncle Edward and other objectionable persons.

But Gerald soon wearied of contemplation. He turned to his

Poem, a composition unrestricted by the boundaries of a single sheet of paper, an interminable Rhyme, second only in importance to St. Sebastian's portrait. Daily he wrote a number of stanzas, celebrating such features of the painting as happened to appeal to him at the moment. His rough copy he wrote on toilet paper, on account of the cheapness of that material; his fair copy he wrote in a round, clear hand on sheets of paper of a size uniform with that of the painting. Some twenty completed sheets lay on the table beside him now.

Today, Gerald decided, he would celebrate in verse the four Sins. Taking the roll of paper and a pencil, he frowned and began to think. At the end of five minutes he had written:

"His sins they were of Carmine Dye,
But now they are as White as Snow."

It was a sound, if not strikingly original, start. He paused again, and wrote down a number of words that rhymed with Dye and Snow,—lie, sye, my, cry, tie, and bow, know, tow, go,—there were lots of them. The problem was now merely to fill in the lines as best suited the sense of the Poem.

After a quarter of an hour's hard thinking Gerald had consumed a yard or so of paper with trials and errors and composed the following verse:

"His Sins they were of Carmine Dye,
But now they are as White as Snow,
Though they were Pink like Strawbry Pye,
They have become as Clean as Dow.

He copied this out in his best handwriting on the fair sheet and wrote 'Verse 42' in the margin. It wasn't his best verse, but it would do in a pinch.

The Poem, though it was named after St. Sebastian and composed in his honour, contained observations upon every mortal thing that Gerald had encountered or imagined in all his eleven years of life, from the peculiar wart alongside his aunt's nose to the mysterious adventures of her false teeth, from the atrocious behaviour of Dorothy's fictitious sweetheart to the monotony of rice pudding every day for lunch. It celebrated the birth of Gerald, who had descended from heaven upon a blue sledge drawn by reindeer, the decease of bad Uncle Stephen and his journey hell-wards on the back of a flaming cayman, the unaccountable behaviour of the chiming clock after Gerald had imprisoned a weevil in it, and the entire calendar of St. Sebastian's mythological adventures, beginning at birth and ending with hara-kiri and arrows.

The Poem, Gerald believed, was a kind of masterpiece, not very good poetry, perhaps, but an important chronicle. Taken together with the Portrait, it was a work of note, an achievement.

He took all the sheets of the Poem, sorted them into their proper order, put the picture of St. Sebastian at the beginning as the frontispiece, and proceeded to bind the book by driving brass paper-clips through the pages. When this was done he laid the book on his lap and looked out of the window.

The breeze was freshening. Little gusts of wind were acreep upon the gravel paths, stirring the yellow dust in whirlpools. The long, lemon-starred fronds of the forsythia bush were waving to and fro; the daffodils were nodding as though they would break their necks. Wispy, shredded flecks of clouds were scudding up from the horizon. Gerald, watching the almond blossom, thought that the flowers looked like a drift of dainty pink shells tossing in a turbulent blue ocean. The wind, still rising, made the curtains into sails and blew showers of petals into the room, tumbling them in little flocks across the green carpet.

The window on the other side of the room stood open, admitting a draught. He pulled the eider-down about his shoulders.

Presently a violent gust of wind swept by him, lifted the Book and tossed it clean out of the window. The flimsy sheets fluttered along the lawn and came to rest under one of the almond trees, where the wind continued to play with them, threatening at any moment to catch them up and fling them beyond the boundary hedge and far away.

Gerald raised himself on his hand and leaned forward to see

where St. Sebastian had gone. A look of anguish came into his face, the bright patches on his cheeks grew pale.

"Auntie, auntie," he shouted.

Not a sound came from the house.

"Dorothy, Dorothy,"

Still there was no answer.

He scowled and gritted his teeth. Flinging off the eider-down, he put his left hand on the floor, then slid his left leg over the edge of the couch till it touched the carpet. A small thud — he was in too great a hurry to lower himself gently — and he was lying on the floor.

He managed to get onto his hands and his knees, and started to crawl towards the French window. Now and then a little stab of pain would shoot through him, and he could feel the drag of the dressing where it stuck to the wound. He was amazed to find how weak he was.

With a great effort he reached up to the handle of the French door and opened it. Down the step and across the crazy paving of the loggia he crawled. The stones were quite hot, he noticed, and strewn with almond blossom. But his eyes were upon the Book, a dozen yards away.

As he crawled over the gravel path, sharp little stones and grit embedded themselves in the palms of his hands.

He was getting weaker. All the strength seemed to be ebbing from his thighs, and his arms felt so flabby that when he reached the lawn he was obliged to lie down for a minute in the damp, cool grass. The wind blew his dressing-gown almost over his head, flapped the tail of his night-shirt, and blew his hair into his eyes. He was cold, but in his anxiety he did not notice it.

The Book frisked about as though there were life in it, and began to mount the hedge. Gerald drove his fingers into the soil, despairing.

But as the wind dropped for a moment, the Book fell onto the grass again, and Gerald became possessed of a new energy. Slowly, like a cat stalking a sparrow, he squirmed along, pushing with his bed-socked feet and pulling at the grass with his hands, never taking his eyes off his quarry.

At length, after what seemed an age, he got within reach of the papers and put out his hand to grasp them. But another gust whipped them away from him. He lay still and sobbed a little as he watched St. Sebastian tumbling about in the air over his head, then making straight for the next-door garden.

Then, with sudden caprice, the wind flung St. Sebastian head-foremost onto the grass right in front of Gerald's nose. Frantically he clutched the papers and held them fast.

Heaving a sigh of infinite happiness he rolled over onto his back.

He saw the almond blossom swaying merrily above him, the black boughs framing shapes of sky incredibly blue, a snow-white sea-gull sailing across them. Now and then he felt the falling pink cups tickle his face and his hands, and his legs where they were bare.

He began to laugh. A petal fell into his mouth and this made him laugh more and more. The red patches showed on his cheeks again and his whole body was convulsed with laughter. He laughed and laughed till the pain of his wound made him cry. Then he laughed again, wildly, uproariously, while the almond blossom tumbled all about him.

Two minutes later his aunt came running along, frantic and weeping.

She found him lying on his back under the almond tree, sprinkled with pink petals. The tears were running down either side of his face onto the grass, and he was laughing as though he would never be able to stop. And clasped firmly against his chest was the portrait of St. Sebastian.

* * *

Chapter 11

The Peach

I

After breakfast John Sampson sat in the easy chair by the fire reading a book about banking. He was studying for an examination.

The room was small and ornate. Over nearly every inch of it were scattered flowers — flowers loose and confined in baskets, flowers rustic and conventional, flowers of all sizes and species. The wall-paper was covered with them, rows and rows of green dog-roses sprouting from little silver waste-paper baskets, that ascended from floor to ceiling with hideous regularity. That part of the floor which was not occupied by the reproduction Persian carpet was preserved from plainness by a covering of linoleum that had evidently been designed in the hope that the eye, if not the foot, would mistake it for a flower-bed. Nor was the ceiling bare. Between the leafy cornice and the mass of filigree that occupied the centre of the ceiling, the plaster was adorned with ornamental paper. From whatever point one looked at the flowers on this paper, one saw patches where the flowers shone silver on a dark ground, and other patches where the flowers were dark and the background silver. It was like a series of negatives and positives of the same unlovely photograph. And the white tablecloth, upon which were scattered the remains of a meal for three people, was like the ceiling.

John Sampson looked up from his book and glared at the wall paper, the floor and the ceiling. They offended him. His mother's taste was, he felt, awful. As the home of a bank clerk this place left a lot to be desired, he told himself.

Presently there came two faint knocks at the door, and the servant girl walked in carrying a tray. Sampson, pretending to read his book, watched her clear the things away from the table.

She was very pretty, he decided for the hundredth time. Her tiny red mouth was made to be covered with kisses. Her black eyes were appealing. Already, though she was only seventeen, her bodice bulged in a way that he found almost irresistible.

Sampson raised his hand from his lap and rested it on the outside of the arm of the chair. As the girl walked round the table she passed his chair, brushing against his hand. Sampson watched her back closely as she swept up the crumbs from the tablecloth. She seemed to be trembling. Then with a swift movement, she turned and faced him, with blushing cheeks. She looked at him intensely, almost accusingly, as she walked towards the door. Again, when passing his chair, her dress brushed against his hand. For a moment, so that the delay scarcely seemed intentional, she lingered and he could feel the warmth and pressure of her body.

Along the hall came the hurrying footsteps of Mrs Sampson, John Sampson's mother.

"Hurry up, hurry up," she cried, in a nagging voice, almost before she had opened the door.

"Get the table-cloth off. Quick now!"

"Yes'm," murmured the girl, timidly, and they folded the cloth.

When they had finished the girl took up the loaded tray and carried it out of the room.

"Wash up the things and no dawdling now," Mrs Sampson cried after the retreating child.

John Sampson saw his mother's red face and the set of her mouth, and decided to go upstairs.

On the first floor he lingered. He looked down into the hall, leaning over the balustrade and listening. There was no sound except the faint clatter of dishes as the girl put them into the washing-up bowl. He walked softly along the passage to the back bedroom, turned the handle, and went in.

The room was tiny and meanly furnished. It contained a single bed garnished with brass pillars and draped with a counterpane that revealed only the palimpsest of a pattern which many washings had nearly removed. Under the window stood a painted dressing table on which lay a brush and comb, a photograph in a tin frame and two discarded face cream jars containing hair slides and buttons. A couple of chairs, with their cane seats broken and frayed, stood against the wall.

He wandered round the room aimlessly, looking at everything and searching for nothing. On one of the chairs lay a neat heap of underclothes, belonging to the girl. These he took up one by one, unfolded them, held them up, walked to the window and examined them, folding and replacing them afterwards. Then he peeped into the chest of drawers, rummaging among the clothes and carefully putting back everything as he found it.

The photograph caught his eye. It was a snapshot of a fisherman clad in a dark jersey. His face, swarthy, pleasant and un-English looking, was surmounted by a cap with a shiny peak, and he wore ear-rings. His hands were thrust deep into his pockets which were placed, not at the sides, but in front of his trousers. The man, Sampson concluded, was the girl's father.

He turned round, rested his arms on the iron bar at the foot of the bed and gazed at the counterpane.

"No," he said to himself, "not on my own door-step. No, it can't be done.

He pictured the girl lying in bed.

Then with a shake of the head he pulled himself together.

"I can't foul my own doorstep," he muttered, and went downstairs again.

After the washing-up was done, Mr and Mrs Sampson, their son, and the servant went into the front room for morning prayers. They all walked up to the bookcase, got out their bibles, sat down and found the chapter for the day.

Mr Sampson, who was a member of the Seamen's Bethel—a little chapel that stood at the back of the fish docks—had commenced years before to read the bible through from cover to cover, a chapter for each morning. At the Bethel, on Sunday afternoons, they did the same thing, with this difference: at the Bethel certain chapters—those that were no more than lists of names and those that dealt with embarrassing subjects—were omitted, but Mr Sampson, in his daily reading, left out nothing. He said each chapter was spiritually profitable.

Today the chapter was from the Book of Jeremiah. Mr Sampson read the woeful prophet's words in an appropriately lugubrious and earnest voice, while no one but himself paid any attention.

The son made no pretence of following the reading. His eyes rested on his father. It was a round, kind, stupid face, in the centre of which there grew a big moustache that always collected pieces of food. Sometimes it was smeared with egg yolk; at other times tea dripped from it. With a microscope it would have been possible to detect the nature of his previous meal from the remnants clinging to its hairs.

Mrs Sampson sat next to him, staring fixedly at her bible, mechanically following every word while she thought about the thing in the oven. She had a thin red face, in which her mouth appeared as straight as if it had been cut with the aid of a ruler and sewn up again, leaving her quite lipless.

John Sampson glanced surreptitiously, without turning his head, at the servant girl, in her black dress and a white cap and apron, sitting on his left. Guardedly too she returned his glance, and their eyes met for an instant. A look of understanding seemed to pass between them.

When Mr Sampson had finished reading he shut his bible, dropped on his knees in front of his chair, rested his elbows on the seat and propped up his head on his hands, while the others followed suit. John Sampson found himself quite close to the girl.

The father began his daily extempore prayer. Every day he prayed for the same things: for the succour of all God's needy and distressed people, for the conversion of many poor souls to Christ, for the family's relatives, for spiritual help for themselves throughout the day. Though the burden of his prayer was always the same, the order of the requests varied from day to day, and small changes were introduced in their wording whenever Mr Sampson picked up a new expression from the Bethel. Long years of practice had given him the ability to talk to his God with the ease and familiarity with which he addressed his wife or his dog. But he was perfectly sincere.

These daily prayers irritated John Sampson to distraction. Derisively he contemplated his father's huge behind, thrust out toward him. Then, having made sure that his mother's face, of which he had a side view, was firmly encased in her hands, he turned to the girl kneeling beside him. With great caution he extended his arm till his hand touched hers lightly. It was as though a powerful current passed through them at the touch, exciting their whole bodies. Her hand closed gently over the tips of his fingers. Timidly and slowly she drew his hand towards her bodice and let it rest there, while Mr Sampson's voice droned monotonous and unheard.

At length the son withdrew his hand, as the father concluded: "In the blessed and worthy name of Our Lord Jesus Christ, Amen."

John Sampson got up, stretched himself, walked into the hall, put on his hat and coat and went out.

Outside, in the main street, everyone was brisk and bustling, enlivened by the sharp sunny winter's day. Humming to himself, Sampson strode along, past whistling errand boys, early housewives armed with shopping baskets, and business men on their way to work.

After ten minutes' walk he came to the bank, a portly, officious looking building. The first person he met inside was Finch, the fellow who worked next to him.

"I say," said Sampson brightly, "our maid's hot stuff."

"Now then, what have you been up to?" replied Finch, wagging his finger and leering.

"Do you think I should be such a fool as to do anything about it?" said Sampson, not a little annoyed at the other's insinuation.

"No, no, no, old man," said Finch in a conciliatory tone, "of course not. You can't do things like that. Not with that kind of person I mean. Impossible."

"No, quite impossible," said Sampson, now soothed.

"Besides, it's far too dangerous. Never can tell the consequences."
"All the same," he added, "she's a perfect peach. Pity she's a servant."

And the two young men laughed, wagging their heads at one another.

II

The months went by. The first crocuses flourished and faded. The Spring came, filling the gardens of the houses with the delightful scents of hyacinths and narcissi, and the young folks began walking in the country lanes of an evening, to hear the nightingales singing.

Soon the Spring was over and the hot sun beat down on the burning pavements and parched the thirsty gardens. The whole town shimmered in a haze of heat that even the sultry sea breezes could not dispel.

In Mrs Sampson's kitchen the air was stifling. The warmth of the stove added to her discomfort. Beads of sweat glistened all over her forehead like dew, and her face became so red that you would have guessed that the blood had congealed just beneath her skin in a hard, shiny layer. As she kneaded the flour in her cooking basin she bent forward, making little furious noises behind her tightly closed lips, noises that she often made when she was alone, or her husband or the maid were in the room.

Her large hands clutched at the sticky masses of flour, working at the stuff as though they were executing punishment for some crime.

She looked up at the cooking stove.

"Come here at once," she shouted, "and put some more coal on this fire."

The girl came in from the scullery, wiping her hands on a dishcloth. She stood on the rag carpet in front of the fire, shovelling coal from the scuttle and pitching it into the grate.

Edith Sampson looked on. Presently the hands ceased writhing and remained still, in the middle of the dough. The woman seemed to stop breathing as she stared at the girl, standing in front of the fire. Then she began to speak, forcing the words through her half closed lips.

"Are you going to have a baby?"

The girl turned to her mistress with a frightened, yet defiant look.

"No," she said breathlessly.

"Come here," said the woman, "let me look at you."

The girl approached, shaking and crestfallen.

Edith Sampson put out her hand, still covered with flour, in the direction of the girl.

"Take you hands off me," she cried angrily. But the woman was stronger and held her by the shoulder, while she passed her hand over the girl's stomach, smearing her dress with dough.

"I thought so," said Mrs Sampson, after she had finished feeling the girl. She spoke hoarsely. "All stayed up to hide it from me."

"It's a lie," moaned the girl, who had begun to cry.

"Very well then," said her mistress, "take off your clothes and let me see."

"I won't."

"Oh, won't you, we'll see about that." and she seized the girl.

At first she resisted, hitting out at the woman's body with her hands. Then, as it became clear that struggle was useless, she gave in.

The elder woman knelt down in front of the younger, and wiped her hands on her apron. She lifted up the girl's dress and undid her stays, grunting as she did so. The girl stood quite still, gulping and wild eyed, while the woman's hands worked beneath her dress. Then the corsets fell on the rug.

A convulsive shudder shook the girl when she felt the touch of the hands on her flesh. With a cry she drew back, but the woman's other hand gripped her leg and held it as though in a vice. All over the stomach the hand worked, feeling and pressing the flesh. Then Edith Sampson lifted the dress and looked at the girl's body, and let her go.

Edith Sampson remained on her knees, gasping,

"Under my roof... Under my roof ... You whore!"

At that the girl looked up.

"You dirty liar," she screamed, crouching forward, thrusting her little tear stained face in front of the woman's. "You stinking hypocrite. You had... You filthy monster, how dare you say a thing like that to me."

She picked up her corsets and ran up to her bedroom. Her mistress followed, shouting,

"You whore... Get out... Get out."

The woman opened the drawers herself, taking out the girl's clothes in handfuls and flinging them into a suitcase, while the girl put on her coat and hat.

"Who did it?" cried Mrs Sampson. Her face was purple, as though she were about to have a fit.

"I won't tell you," said the girl, somewhat calmer now.

The woman threw the photograph into the suitcase and shut the lid.

"Get out at once," she cried, towering over the girl and threatening her with clenched fists.

The girl dried her eyes, lifted her heavy bag and carried it downstairs, swinging it against the balusters, while the woman followed at her heals.

"Strumpet!" she hissed in the girl's ear as she went out at the front door.

Dazed, struggling with her burden, she walked down the garden path and into the street.

III

Next morning, at the bank, when the cashier had gone into the manager's room, Sampson said to Finch in a whisper,

"You know that servant I told you about?"

"Ah," replied Finch.

"Well, she's having a baby."

"No!" Finch exclaimed.

"Yes. Mother discovered it yesterday morning and turned her out of the house."

"Good Lord!" said Finch, "anything to do with you?"

"No it isn't," answered Sampson angrily. "Do you think I'm crazy?"

"Sorry," Finch said, "only pulling your leg. But tell me how it happened."

"I tell you," Sampson whispered to his friend, "all I ever did was to touch her now and then. You know how it is. She was damned attractive, a peach. But I never spoke to her, never kissed her. She would have taken advantage of it. It would have led her to other things and then I might have been saddled with her for life. So we went on like that till yesterday. Then when I got home she was gone and my mother told me about it."

"Who was it then?" asked Finch, overbrimming with curiosity.

"That's where this note comes in." Sampson produced from his pocket a scrap of paper. "Here, read it for yourself."

Finch took it and read:

"I did it because you wouldn't speak to me and be kind. It was only you I was thinking of. He is going to marry me, my father made him, but I shall always think of you."

There was nothing more, no heading and no signature.

"Well I'll be damned," said Finch, handing back the note, "What an ass you were!"

Sampson stroked his little waxed moustache.

"Yes," he said, "I was a perfect ass. If only I'd known before." Then he paused and said, as much to himself as to his friend,

"To think that for all those months I never did anything to her, and she in love with me. All those wasted months. There was that other fellow, probably some fisherman or other, ready to take her when things became obvious, and no risk of landing myself with a kid to keep." Sampson sighed with regret.

"What an ass I was to be sure. It would have been as safe as houses and as easy as winking."

"She ought to have told you," said Finch, "After all, she was in love with you."

"I know," answered Sampson. A broad grin spread over his features.

"What fun it would have been. Night after night for months and months. She was such a peach. Every night…"

The cashier's head appeared behind his glass screen, and the two young men bent down over their work, chuckling softly and winking at one another.

* * *

Chapter 12

Red Front!

Aquinas Street lay somewhat to the east of Camden Town High Street, and it had once been respectable. Now all the houses were let off into tenements of one, two, or at the most three rooms to each family. During the day hordes of grimy children played in the gutters and on the pavement; costers pushed their barrows along, ringing bells and shouting; barrel-organs played melancholy tunes; mothers leaned out of windows and screeched at their children, telling them to cease fighting one another or to get out of the roadway because of the traffic. The facade of the houses, dusky and foul as though the dirt laden atmosphere were constantly congealing on its surface, stretched from end to end of the street in an unbroken plane, relieved only by windows, lace curtained, newspaper curtained and un-curtained, at regular intervals. On Friday and Saturday nights sounds of revelry used to come from some of the rooms, the jingling notes of a piano and raucous voices singing popular songs. Often, sometimes two or three times a day, a handcart stood outside one of the houses and miserable sticks of furniture were brought down from one of the tenements and wheeled away.

On the third floor of one of the houses, at the top of a bare, creaking staircase, the cleaning of which appeared to be no-one's business, there was a large room where Yallop lived.

Even at noonday, and however brilliantly the sun shone outside, it was twilight in this room, on account of the smallness of the window. The architect who had designed the street a hundred years before had been a great scholar of classical architecture and a disciple of Palladio, consequently, for the sake of exterior correctness, the top floors of all the houses had been provided with apertures very much like loop-holes, in place of windows, as though the place had been a prison. Inside, the glass was fly-blown; outside, it was covered with a brown deposit that had been washed into little puddles and rivulets by the rain. To further darken the room, wads of newspaper had been stuffed into holes in the glass. Incredible as it may seem, these obstructions were not enough. Though the window was not overlooked, it was impossible to see more than a few inches into the room from the opposite side of the street, the festoons of a heavy lace curtain covered all but a tiny triangle of glass, and this triangle was blocked by a miserable dust-laden fern in a pink earthenware pot. The room might as well have been a subterranean cave and its tenant a troglodyte.

Though it was a cold, damp, foggy November day outside, there was no fire in the grate. The weather indoors, in fact, was as cold and as damp and as foggy as it was in the street. A pungent smell of sweat and old clothes filled the room. If it had been possible to see at all, you would have noticed that the walls had once been papered with shiny brown paper of the kind that is found in the halls of Victorian villas. All round the room, as high as a man could reach, ran a kind of dado composed of small stains, each marking the spot where a bug had been squashed beneath a thumbnail. By the window, where the wet had penetrated the wall, the paper hung down in folds, revealing greyish white patches of plaster, spotted with blue mould like a corpse. A great iron bedstead, propped up with a packing-case where one of the legs had broken, occupied the centre of the floor opposite the fireplace. The rest of the furniture comprised a pair of rickety wooden chairs, a table, and a chest of drawers with a missing foot. The mantelshelf over the stove was loaded with all manner of oddments—knives and forks and spoons, cups and saucers, newspapers, a hairbrush and a clock that was out of order. The only covering that the floor boards could boast was a square of wretched drugget by the bed.

Yallop sat reading by the window, holding up his book to catch the last feeble gleams of light that filtered through the curtain before dark came. He was a young man, with a grey tired face and a hulk of a body that was suffering from lack of exercise. His clothes were the colour of dirt, his face was unshaven and he hadn't worn a collar and tie since he had lost his job two years ago.

Those had been comfortable happy days, when he and his wife had lived in a little house with a garden and he had worked in the engineering shop, earning good money. Soon after their daughter was born he lost his job and the landlord evicted them. First they lived with her mother in Stepney, then they came to Aquinas Street. All the work he had done since he left the factory was to shovel up some snow the previous winter.

Then a month ago, Phyllis, his wife, had died. Heart failure, the doctor said it was. But Yallop knew that if they had been living at the cottage in Dagenham, and he in work, she would have stayed as hale and as happy as she had been on the day he married her. He told himself that the employer who had given him the sack had murdered her.

When Yallop thought of this he was not very angry. He was sullen. Fine feelings like love and hatred and pride got watered down in Aquinas Street; they smouldered but they did not flame. Since the days of the Dagenham cottage, the only desire that had burnt steadily in Yallop's heart had been for a joint of meat in the cupboard and a heap of coals in the grate, with a job of work to make them possible. Today there was neither, and the prospect for tomorrow was a gloomy one. He felt in his pocket and found a half a crown and two pennies. And there were three days to go before the Public Assistance Committee would give him more.

When his wife had died, Yallop began to go to political meetings and march in demonstrations of the unemployed. There he was told that it was not necessary that his wife should have died, and that it was possible for men to live without factory owners who could sack you as they pleased. He was also told that he 'had nothing to lose but his chains.'

Yallop didn't understand all that the communists told him, but sufficient to arouse his interest. On the very day after his wife's funeral—a pauper's funeral—he had heard a fierce eloquent Scotchman talk from a platform. He had spoken about fine idle ladies who gave their dogs meals consisting of dainties and delicate cooked meats, and told how they thought nothing of spending a hundred pounds on a fur coat and bought half a dozen hats a week. There was many a man, the speaker said, who had never worked at all but nevertheless spent as much on one banquet with his friends as a poor woman would spend on food in a whole year. And why? Because his father had been so-and-so the great merchant, or what's-his-name the crafty lender of money; or because his grandfather had married for money rather than for love. The Scotchman went on to describe two babies, one the child of a rich man, the other of a poor man. You couldn't tell the difference between them. Perhaps the rich baby had better brains, bigger capacities; perhaps it hadn't. It was impossible to tell. Why was it, then, that one should have nurses and good food and a beautiful home and expensive schooling and everyone bowing down before him as soon as he could toddle, while the other existed in a place that you wouldn't stable a horse in, ate food that a farmer wouldn't give to cattle, went to a school where he was taught that the world is practically as God intended it to be, and little else, and was finally thrown out into the world where he had the choice between helping to support the other boy, and starvation? Why was it possible? Because Yallop and all the other poor folk allowed it to be so. But it wasn't necessary. There were other ways of doing things.

One of his new friends lent Yallop a book about Russia, where, he was told, such things did not happen. Yallop, having read the daily newspapers, had the impression that Russia was a dreadful place where every year half the population died of hunger and the other half were shot for political reasons. It was also, he gathered, a terribly powerful country with millions of efficient soldiers and thousands of aeroplanes, a menace to civilization. He had also read an article in a magazine, written by a man whose brother had a friend who had once spent a week in Moscow. The revelations were very terrible indeed.

But this book that he was reading told a different story. It was all about the wonderful goings-on in October 1918, when the poorest people took control of everything. The part he liked best of all was about the burial of the dead comrades in the Brotherhood Grave. He could see it all very clearly in his mind: snow on the ground and on the roofs; splendid colourful domes like monstrous turnips soaring up into the sky—a fairyland scene like the view eastwards from the bridge in St. James' Park, but with more brilliant colours. He saw great multitudes of strange men and women in the streets. He saw the crowds thronging into the vast Red Square, singing and shouting and waving red banners. Then the endless, tireless procession of soldiers and factory workers bearing red-draped coffins made of rough wood and the weeping men and women; the burial of the comrades who had died in the great common grave, and the solemn singing of the Internationale. Thousands upon thousand of comrades, marching all day through the mighty square, coming in by the Iberian Gate and leaving by way of the Nikolskaya. It was wonderful. Christ! If he had only been among them!

And Russia now? The book told him about all the new factories, the tractors and the aeroplanes, new cities springing up in the middle of the steppe, the wonderful new Russia that they were building. And it all belonged to the working men and women. There weren't any unemployed in this country of the soviets, or very rich people. Everyone had the right to work and eat. They didn't pamper lap dogs and starve children.

And why shouldn't the English workers do the same? A Soviet Britain! Sometimes it seemed hopeless; people were so callous and afraid. But when he read about Russia, or listened to a thrilling speech at a meeting, or marched in a demonstration, then a Soviet Britain seemed not so far away.

Long after it had become quite dark, Yallop sat crouched in his chair by the window, thinking about Russia. The lamp in the street cast a faint lozenge of light on the ceiling, forming a sort of halo about the shadow of his head. He leaned back and watched the feeble beams of light that travelled across the ceiling, this way and that, as an occasional car went by. Somewhere not far away a scratchy gramophone was playing, and the folks underneath were having a violent quarrel.

There came a small sound from the bed. Yallop got up and groped about among the things on the mantelpiece. He found the butt end of a candle, lit it, and went over to the bed.

In the middle of the pillow, which was grey all over, lay the head of his daughter, a girl of five years. Her skin was white and delicate and seemed all the fairer because of the mass of curling red hair that tumbled all around it, half covering the loathsome pillow; and her mouth was a little scarlet oval. As he came near she opened her eyes: deep brown eyes they were, big like her mother's had been.

By God, she reminded him of Phyllis! Phyllis, whose head had lain there on that very pillow only four weeks ago, dead. Her hair had been just like that, and though her face was so thin her skin had been as white and her eyes as brown. Only, her lips were white too and cold, as though all the blood had drained out of her. She had died suddenly in the night, without any sound. He had touched her arm and found it cold, cold, and then her forehead, and that was as cold as a stone. It was a terrible thing to find her like that. Frantically he had shaken her, but her body was limp and cold. He got out of bed trembling, scarcely daring to look at her. Her eyes were open. He couldn't believe she was dead. And then, on the pillow, just at the edge of her beautiful red hair, he had seen a little brown thing. It was that which made his grief articulate. A bug… and there she was, dead…

He stood with the candle in his hand looking at the girl, full of resentment against the world. She was so different from the rest of the children in Aquinas Street, so much more beautiful, a strange flower blooming in that squalid atmosphere. After her mother had died she hadn't been very well. But she would mend. They wouldn't take his girl too!

She gave him a wan little smile.

"Ow yr feelin' now?" he asked her.

"All right."

"I'm goin' out. Call Mrs Stubb if yer want anythink."

Mrs Stubb was the woman who lived in the room underneath. She had four children of her own and she drank a good deal, but she was a mighty kind woman.

He went to the chest of drawers and hunted for something—a rag. He couldn't find one, so he tore a long strip of cloth off an old shirt and came back to the bed.

Last night, when he was out, a bug had got into the child's ear. It wouldn't happen tonight, he'd make certain of that. Tightly he bound the rag over her ears, under her chin and over the top of her head, muttering to himself.

Crossing to the door, he took the cloth cap that hung there and put it on, and a scarf that had once been white, and wrapped it round his neck.

"So long," he said, blew out the candle and went out, locking the door behind him.

On his way down he knocked at Mrs Stubb's door. Mrs Stubb opened it. Her haggard, violent face bobbed about on a level with his stomach.

"Orf agen!" she said, "why the 'ell can't yer look arter yer own bloody kid?"

He gave her the key.

"Just in caise she wants anythink," he said.

Mrs Stubb took the key and slammed the door.

Mrs Stubb was a strange creature, always cursing people, and the more she cursed them the more she did for them. Many a bit of food she had taken up to the girl when Yallop was out, and said nothing about it. The only flowers that his wife had had at her funeral had come from Mrs Stubb and they had been expensive artificial ones. Her husband was often in work to be sure, but considering the amount they drank it was wonderful how she did it. Another funny thing about Mrs Stubb was the way she sent her two eldest off to Sunday School every Sunday afternoon, cursing and swearing at them (as like as not she was drunk) till they went, then going to great trouble to find out from other children who lived in the street if they really had been, or had merely been mucking about in the next street.

Yallop clumped down the dark staircase, that threatened to give way at every step, and found himself in the street. It was chill and damp but the fog had lifted. He turned up the collar of his jacket, thrust his hand in his pocket, and struck out for St Pancras.

After ten minutes he came to the great railway arches that span the road at the back of St Pancras Station. A funereal place this, with its huge bastions of grey brick and immense girders soaring overhead and impenetrable shadows. Everything looked colossal, deathly, drained of all vestige of colour save for orange circles cast on the ground by infrequent street lamps, and an occasional tramcar, brilliantly lit, that sailed swiftly by.

Many dim figures were standing about in the shadows, some in groups talking in low voices, some singly, lounging against the wall of the bridge. Most of them were men with cloth caps and no collars like Yallop, grey, sullen looking men. There were a few women, dowdy, yet smarter than the men. And there was a group of young fellows in flannel trousers and tweed jackets, with great mufflers round their necks, smoking and talking excitedly. They were students. Some of them carried banners, long bamboo poles with little glittering hammer-and-sickle emblems at the top, and furled red cloth. One young fellow went round with a bundle of newspapers, offering them to the bystanders and shouting:

"Daily Worker one penny. Buy the worker's only newspaper!"

He came to where Yallop stood leaning against the wall. He was a bright fair-headed youth and he spoke as university men speak:

"Daily Worker, Comrade?"

Yallop shook his head.

"'Ow long till they start?" he asked.

"Soon now," replied the student, who was evidently enjoying himself. "There's a crowd of mounted cops round the corner, waiting for us." Then he pointed to two men who stood on the other side of the road, their faces invisible in the darkness.

"See those two fellows?" said the young man.

"Ah."

"They're spies, copper's narks. One of them—the fat one in a bowler—went to a meeting in Finsbury the other night and somebody handed a note up to the chairman saying that there was a police spy in the hall, but not saying who it was. The chairman—it was Ralph Fox, who had been the friend of Lenin—got up and asked the spy to go, whoever he was. The crowd was furious, but the fellow in the bowler sat tight, not winking an eyelid. Then it leaked out who it was and the people round him made things so hot that he got up and tried to go. But they wouldn't let him. Fox got up and asked them to let him go and not to soil their fingers by touching him. At last he got away, but not before someone had landed him one on the jaw. They smuggled out the chap who had done the hitting by dressing him up in someone else's clothes, and the cops waiting for him at the door didn't get him."

"Ah. I know all about that," said Yallop, "it was me that hit him."

"Was it though!" said the youth, "I felt like it myself. Don't blame you."

By this time the crowd had begun to form itself into a straggling file, four deep, at the side of the road, and Yallop and the youth took up their places towards the end of the procession.

The leader was a little old man well known in revolutionary circles, a Parsee, with a yellowish skin, dressed in European clothes and carrying an old umbrella. He was reputed to have been immensely rich and to have spent nearly all his money on the Cause. Yallop had once heard him deliver a rousing speech about the dreadful things that went on in India, under the British flag.

Behind the Parsee stood a young woman with a red scarf, holding a great red banner, beautifully embroidered with a picture of Lenin in the middle and some Russian characters underneath. The communists were very proud of this banner, which had been presented by the workers of a factory in Leningrad to their British comrades.

The Russians who gave it had been sure that before very long Britain would be a Soviet State.

The body of the procession was made up of all sorts of people of all ages, but Yallop, who towered above them all, could see that most of them wore cloth caps, were working men.

Someone in the front ranks had a kettle drum, and began to sound a ratatoo on it. Suddenly, as if the beating of the drum were the cue for their appearance, a posse of mounted police armed with sword-sticks, trotted out of the side street and rode up to the file of demonstrators. Two of them took up a position at the head of the column, in front of the Parsee, while the rest guarded the right flank at intervals, and brought up the rear. Twenty foot police appeared like magic and attached themselves to the demonstration. One of them, a fellow as tall as Yallop, stood next to him. Catcalls, boos and ironical cheers rose from the ranks and Yallop muttered a word that made the policeman at his side start and instinctively finger his baton.

The leader shouted "Quick march!" and the procession moved forward, all out of step, in the direction of Euston Road, while the drummer attempted to beat time. A great white horse a few paces in front of Yallop began to rear. He remembered that someone had told him about the way to discomfort these mounted police: scatter marbles in the road, and the horses would slide about everywhere, or a wire stretched across the road wrought wonderful havoc when they charged. A sudden hatred welled up in him, so that he was sorely tempted to tackle the policeman that walked by his side. Just a little shove, rightly timed, and he would be under the wheels of the tram which was at that moment coming up from behind! Yallop recollected having seen a poor old man's head all bloody from a blow with a police baton, during a demonstration in Hyde Park. The old chap had sworn that he had been drinking a cup of tea at a refreshment booth when the police had charged and cracked him on the scull. Devils, these police!

They were drawing near to the main road when Yallop spied,

chalked up on the wall that ran alongside the pavement, the words: "Down with the Baby-starving Boss Government." Straggling and ill fashioned the letters were, but he regarded them with pride, for they were his own handiwork. The night before, he and another comrade had written them up, while two more kept guard to warn them if the police should come. They did come, and Yallop had escaped by running into a side street and hiding in a recess. The copper had run straight on and missed him.

At the corner the police held up the demonstration for a minute to let the traffic pass. Then they marched into the broad busy thoroughfare, where the pavements were thronged with people. Yallop noticed with what surprise and distaste many of them regarded the banners and the marching men, surrounded with police like a gang of convicts. He imagined the better dressed of them quaking with fear of revolutions. By cripes! it was heartening to march under a red banner! It made him feel as though victory were near, with so many faithful comrades marching valiantly against the enemy. They were all stepping out bravely now, conscious of the stir they were making. Proudly the young woman held her banner, and the kettle drum tapped bravely.

Then a voice started to sing lustily and a hundred singers joined in, stamping the time with their feet:

> Come workers sing a rebel song,
> A song of love and hate,
> Of love unto the lowly,
> And hatred to the great:
> The great who trod our fathers down,
> Who steal our children's bread,
> Whose hand of greed is laid upon
> The living and the dead.

Yallop, although he had only heard the song once or twice before, sang with zest, throwing up his head. Then came the chorus:

Then sing a rebel song
As we proudly march along
To end the age long tyranny
That makes for human tears;
For our march is nearer done
With each setting of the sun,
And the tyrant's might is passing
With the passing of the years.

It was fine! Especially that bit about human tears appealed to him. That was truly said: they were going to end the age long tyranny that makes for human tears. Ay, it made for human tears right enough. And the bit about the children's bread was true too. His girl lying in bed… the bugs… his wife in her coffin… his whole life, a dog's life. No, worse than that. Many a fine lady's lap-dog…

Splendid cars glided smoothly by, while the occupants peered out at the demonstrators with horrified faces. Yallop hated them. But he no longer cared for himself, or even for his child. To end the age long tyranny… It didn't matter whether you went under in the fight so long as the fight went on. At that moment it seemed to him a desirable thing that he should go under for love of the lowly. Yes, and for hatred of the great!

After they had finished one song they began another. The second was a Russian airmen's song, that Yallop could not follow. It was a strange, rousing song, parts of which were shouted, not sung. In the middle of every verse came the words RED FRONT, which everybody bawled at the top of his voice. Yallop deafened everyone near him. A kind of ecstasy was upon him. His great body swayed along without his noticing it. His mind dwelt upon the fight and the glorious future that they would establish.

Presently they came near to one of the great metropolitan hospitals and the leader shouted a command which Yallop did not hear. Immediately the singing and shouting ceased, and instead they began to whistle the Marseillaise. Yallop wondered for a moment why they had stopped singing, then the meaning of it dawned on him. Ill people lying there… poor people… mustn't be disturbed. Something like a sob was wrung from him for no reason at all when he thought of that gesture of kindness. Coming from revolutionaries it seemed somehow… splendid.

Then, when they had passed the hospital, something glorious happened. They had come to a big square where a contingent of demonstrators from the East End stood waiting for them. As soon as the two companies saw one another a loud shout went up from both of them and there were many cries of "Red Front," and much saluting with raised clenched fists, after the Anti-Fascist manner. The waiting company was a huge one, crimson with banners and surrounded with many police. And it had a band, a small one and a bad one, but it made a wonderful difference. A wild joy seemed to possess the two crowds at their meeting, as the band played, slowly and solemnly, the Internationale. Yallop tore off his cap and sang like a man possessed.

Rough brave fellows, these from the East End, shouting and gesticulating. They were grouped according to their districts and Yallop identified them by their banners. The first group came from Whitechapel: Communist Party Whitechapel, their banner said. Then there were the banners of the Limehouse Branch of the Communist Party, the Stepney International Labour Defence, banners of the National Unemployed Workers' Movement and many more. It was like the Red Square! Had they come in by the Iberian Gate; were they leaving by way of the Nikolskaya? Was that shadow yonder a yawning chasm, the Brotherhood Grave? It might… by Christ, it must have been like this!

The two processions merged into one, with the East End in front and the band in the middle, playing away like fury. On they marched again, to revolutionary music. Every now and then someone on the pavement would fall into the ranks, receiving as he did so a small ovation. Yallop felt that he would like to grasp everyone by the hand and shout 'Comrades!' at the top of his voice. All his life long he had been shut up in himself. He had been small and lonely. Now a wonderful feeling of mystical union with these comrades filled him. The purpose of these men was his steady purpose. There was no feeling to match this in the whole world!

After two miles of marching the procession arrived at its destination, the great Hall, where the speakers were waiting. The police dispersed and disappeared as mysteriously as they had arrived, and the banners were lowered and furled as the stream of men poured itself into the building. In the Hall, the waiting crowds greeted them with cheering.

Yallop found a seat at the back. In front of him, stretching right up to the platform, was a sea of heads, thousands of them. Hundreds more were perched up in the gallery which ran down either side of the Hall. The place was already packed, yet more and more kept arriving. Each contingent sent its banner up to the platform, which was a blaze of red. As each new one arrived a cheer went up from the company. Familiar slogans, painted in red on strips of cloth, were draped along the edge of the balcony and over the stage.

Five men walked onto the platform. Immediately everyone stood up and sang the Internationale, accompanied by a piano that stood near the stage. At the end of the first verse some were for sitting down. After the last verse, one old fellow, in a state of fanatical excitement, began singing yet another verse, but the men on either side made him sit down. Even then he couldn't stop cheering.

The chairman called for silence and the speeches began. Yallop sat leaning forward, straining to catch every word.

The speaker was the leader of the Communist Party of Great Britain, a small round headed man in a brown suit. He talked about War and Fascism and Unemployment, beginning quietly but working himself up into a frenzy towards the end, when he spoke of the heroism of the workers in foreign lands who had suffered imprisonment and torture and death for the sake of socialism and the brotherhood of man.

This part of it Yallop felt he could understand. But the rest — all this talk full of phrases such as 'the struggling masses', 'the ripening

situation', 'Lacqueys of the bourgeoisie', and 'dialectical material-
ism'—was difficult to follow. But he drank in every word as though
it were precious nectar. These men were the workers' leaders; they
would establish the workers' paradise.

At the end of the speech everyone cheered and the fanatical old
man tried to sing the Internationale again.

The next speaker was a white-haired veteran revolutionary, well
known all over the world. He strode up and down the platform,
pounding away at the table, gesticulating, bursting with eloquence.
He was easier to understand, this fellow; he talked in the common
language. A widely read man he was, and full of anecdotes. He had
been in prison a score of times, had fought with the workmen of
Petrograd in '18 and again with the Chinese communists in '25. At
the beginning of his speech he talked about Ruskin, quoting the
words he had written to a friend: I am a communist, the reddest of
the red, and I hate all manner of thieving. Yallop sat spellbound. A
great man, a man of learning was this Ruskin, a professor, and he
had said a thing like that! Yallop felt like cheering. Again, at the end
of his speech the old revolutionary sang—yes, actually sang—in a
great voice that shook a little, the last verse of Jerusalem:

I will not cease from mental fight,
Nor shall my sword sleep in my hand
Till we have built Jerusalem
In England's green and pleasant land.

Yallop found it difficult to keep his seat. He wanted to fight and
spend himself, use his powerful body to build the new Jerusalem.
He clenched his fists and the sweat gathered on his forehead.

Then the collection was taken. A greasy cap, weighted down with
coppers and sixpences, was handed to Yallop. Without hesitation
he produced his halfcrown and flung it into the cap. Half a crown!
For such a Cause, a miserable offering! From this hour on he was
a new man! A man with a goal!

All through the meeting, down to the final Internationale, he thought of nothing else. All the way back to the Arches the words of that song kept ringing in his head…

Having found the key of his room in the corner of the landing, where Mrs Stubb always left it, he unlocked the door and went in. When he had lit the candle he went over to the bed.

The girl turned her bandaged head towards him, squinting because of the light.

"'Ow are yer?" he asked.

"I'm 'ungry."

"Aint Mrs Stubb been up?"

"No."

"I'll get yer sommat."

He was about to go out to buy some food at the delicatessen store at the end of the street when he remembered that the halfcrown had gone.

He sat down on the bed and covered his face with his hands.

"What's the matter?" asked the child, after a time.

There came no answer, only a shaking of the bed, as though he were sobbing.

At length he looked up and cursed vehemently. Cursed himself, and life and the communists with great roaring oaths. He lay back groaning.

Soon they were both asleep, the man lying fully dressed on the bed, with one arm round the girl's head and his hand touching the bandage that bound her hair.

After half an hour the candle on the chest of drawers, having burnt down, guttered and went out, leaving them in darkness.

* * *

Chapter 13

The Crimson Tiger

I

Up from the North came the Crimson Tiger, romping in the night air, his vermeil coat sparkling against the black sky. Gracefully he frisked and lunged, gambolling in a sportive, yet tranquil, mood far above the earth, as is the custom of Crimson Tigers.

Yet he was no ordinary Tiger. Sudden whimsies came upon him, swift longings filled his tigerish soul. He aspired to the glaucous rim of the western sky, where the sun had lately set, and began fitfully to glide thither. Next, espying how pale and cold the stars shone, he essayed to cool his fires in the chilly radiance of Orion and Betelgeuse. Incontinent, he permitted the gentle breath of the West Wind to bear him he knew not whither, to ruffle his crimson fur with her caresses. The moon, so big and white, resting on the horizon, beckoned wantonly to him, but no sooner had she awakened his longing than a rival filled it altogether. The Town, the sweet-scented gardens and lights of the Town, were all his love and desire.

So keen were the eyes of the Crimson Tiger that he could see the roofs of all the houses and every tile upon them, though as yet the moon shone but dimly. He perceived also a certain weather-vane — how he delighted in weather-vanes! — that was, in a manner of speaking, a relative of his. For this weather-vane was also a Tiger, a furbished silver Tiger, a sinewy, brave beast, who could nevertheless prowl no way but round and round about his own middle, so sadly tethered and transfixed he was. But the Crimson Tiger, entranced at the sight of his kinsman, frolicked about him, admiring the glint of the moon along his back as the West Wind lashed him gently, causing him to dart this way and that.

Soon tiring of the Weather-vane Tiger, with his ordered motions, the Crimson Tiger gave a great bound, cleaving the air so that it whistled through his fur, and presently discovered that he was floating over a garden.

Carpeted with the pink and white blossoms of rose bushes and night-scented stocks was this garden. He could see every petal as though it were day, more clearly, in fact, than if the noonday sun had been shining. But chiefly it was their scent which delighted him, which gave him those voluptuous tremors that only Crimson Tigers can properly enjoy. Drunken with the heady perfume, he lurched from side to side, skipped and pranced along the laden air in a pensive blissfulness, dreaming his evening dreams.

He was not alone. A little Flame Shoulder was tumbling about in a tipsy condition among the hollyhocks. A Rosy Footman fell quivering from the sky like a snowflake on a gusty day, and landed right in the middle of the garden path, next to a Hebrew Character who had been reclining there for the space of an hour. But the Crimson Tiger, absorbed in his dreams, took no notice of his companions.

So drowsy he was that he let the West Wind waft him beyond the garden and away over the house-tops. Dancing in his besotted eye, there shone a planet, another moon, a moon girt about with stripes, suspended over the pavement. A flickering light, now blue-cold, now pinkish, now dazzling white, diffused the cross-gartered moon, moving the Crimson Tiger with wonder. He made towards it with lazy movements of his body. It filled his vision as he approached, blinding him with its baleful brilliance. A sinister foreboding made him shudder in all his limbs. The light affected his eyes, yet it was irresistible, fascinating like a serpent. Whichever way he wheeled, it was only the cross-gartered moon that he saw. The night, the Ethiopian darkness of the night that he loved, the odours of those flowers that love the evening also, all crepuscular and nocturnal delights, were gone, swallowed up in the hideous glare of the moon. The Crimson Tiger, like his relative the Weather-vane, was tethered and powerless, condemned by a cruel fate to revolve, as if he were a blood-red comet about a Centre.

How many orbits the Crimson Tiger might have described about the cross-gartered moon, had not his passage been rudely interrupted, it is impossible to say. For in his dizzy flight he did not perceive a snare, a net with mesh so strong, with cords so stout, that no Crimson Tiger that has ever lived could have escaped its toils. It did not move. It lay in wait across the orbit of the Tiger. Utterly unable to change his course, he plunged right into the cavern, down to its furthermost pocket, where his motion was stilled against the cruel mesh, his crimson body bruised, the pride of his soul laid low.

He wheeled about, groping blindly for the door whence he had entered. Madly and vainly he sought to tear the cords, to squeeze his body through the net, to find egress by some hole in the cavern. Losing his wits, he flung himself against the bars again and again, to the great injury of his crimson coat. He was humiliated, vanquished, exhausted, and there was no more spirit left in him.

Shuddering and cowed, he rested, held onto the cords of the net with his claws, and resigned himself to the ways of Providence.

II

The Crimson Tiger lay asleep on a spotless sheet of white blotting-paper. Around him, on the table, were scattered small bottles and trays from Gerald's half-guinea laboratory set (rashly presented by his friend Mr Tetrapod on the occasion of Gerald's thirteenth birthday), some brushes, a box of paints, and the little glass-lidded case in which the Crimson Tiger had spent the greater part of the previous night. Gerald himself sat at the table, alternately regarding the Tiger with admiration, and mixing liquids in a test-tube.

On the blotting-paper, by the side of the Crimson Tiger, there lay a Common White or Cabbage butterfly, stone dead, with a pin through its middle. A miserable, washed-out looking creature it appeared beside the Tiger, and nowise improved by the fact that its wings were stained all over, like a patchwork quilt, with chemicals and daubs of paint. Here and there the cream scales that covered its wings had been rubbed off, revealing the shiny membrane beneath, like the wing of a fly.

Gerald was experimenting. He bent down over the Cabbage White to watch the effect of a drop of liquid that he had just transferred from the test-tube to the butterfly's wing. The result was not at all what he had expected. A brown stain appeared where the drop had fallen, then a hole in the wing, while a wisp of brown vapour arose from the blotting-paper. Gerald swore gently, then began to concoct another, and, as he hoped, less potent dye.

The next attempt was more successful. As the new fluid spread over the wing, it turned a spot, about the size of a pea, to a brilliant viridian. Gerald got up and executed a small dance of delight round the dining table while singing, for some hidden reason, the first verse of the Bay of Biscay, lengthening the final Biscay Oooo into a low whoop of delight that lasted till he was panting for breath. Then he sat down again and shifted the blotting-paper till the Crimson Tiger lay immediately in front of him.

The fore-wings of the Crimson Tiger were rich and lustrous, as though made of very fine plush, and dark brown, almost black, in colour, relieved by a number of large cream spots. Only on summer nights did he deign to reveal the glory of his crimson and black underwings. During the day he concealed them beneath his fore-wings, which he kept drawn back against his body. His shoulders were brown, adorned with long feathery scales; his belly was fat and tender, covered with scarlet fur, banded and spotted with black. In a deep, dreamless slumber he lay, quite oblivious of the fact that if he were at that moment to awake, to spread his wings and fly, he might perchance find the open window, escape, and hide himself from harm among the flowers in the garden. But being a slow-witted Moth, of crepuscular habits and a deep sleeper, he was as surely a captive as if he had been imprisoned in a strong-room, or were dead.

Taking up a fine brush, Gerald dipped it into the test-tube, which contained a greenish liquid. A minute drop hung trembling from the point of the brush. With utmost care he lowered the brush till the drop touched the Crimson Tiger's right fore-wing, just in the centre of the outermost cream spot. As though by magic the subtle fluid spread till it engulfed the spot, turning it a bright metallic green, like the verdigris on a copper dome. Then, again with infinite care, Gerald coloured the corresponding spot on the left wing.

The lily had been gilded with conspicuous success. Gerald considered that he had effected a vast improvement. The Moth was now possessed of a pair of large green eye-spots, a not inappropriate thing, Gerald felt, in a Crimson Tiger. An agreeable thing, an excellent idea, one that should be pursued further!

He put the blotting-paper to one side, in order that the Moth should be out of harm's way, and set out to concoct another dye. Of a strictly empirical nature were Gerald's experiments. His method, if method it can be called, was to mix every liquid, powder and crystal, to mix three, four, five of them in various proportions, to dissolve solids in water or acid, to boil liquids in a test-tube held in a pair of tongs over a candle flame (how he cursed Uncle Edward for denying him a Bunsen burner!), to pulverise crystals in a mortar, to set them alight, to subject everything to every conceivable treatment. Curious things happened. The cardinal virtue of Chemistry, in Gerald's eyes, was that it held innumerable shocks in store for him, like an infinitely versatile Jack-in-the-box. Sometimes a grey and pestilential smoke would arise from the test-tube, or a peculiar gamboge vapour, causing Uncle Edward to complain at meal-times that the room smelt like a sewage disposal works, or a soap factory, or a rotten egg, as the case might be. On other occasions a minor explosion would occur, and Gerald would seek to calm the fears of Aunt Amelia by assuring her that he had merely dropped the large iron tray which he kept by him to serve as a scapegoat for the more unmanageable mixtures.

Gerald's immediate purpose was concerned with the less spectacular demonstrations of Chemical Skill. Desiring to make a dye of another hue, for the further glorification of the Crimson Tiger, he mixed and brewed over the candle a likely compound, with a dash of this, a sprinkling of that, and a drop of the other. But the result was disappointing. The liquid, which was as to colour coffee, as to consistency treacle, boiled violently, emitting clouds of dun-coloured steam that had an evil smell. A drop of the liquid, applied to the Cabbage White, formed a little globule which ran off onto the table, leaving no trace on the wing. New combinations, unprecedented mixtures, gave interesting colours and smells and one slight report, but never a stain that Gerald thought worthy of the Crimson Tiger. Observing the fulness of the slop basin and the relative emptiness of his bottles, Gerald felt half inclined to own himself beaten. But he determined to make one more experiment, the last.

He washed out the test-tube in a jam jar of water, cleaned the candle soot from its surface, and wiped it on a rag. He placed two small crystals in the tube and added about a thimbleful of clear liquid. There appeared, not indeed that royal blue for which he had hoped, but a puce froth. Innumerable puce bubbles mounted the tube, forming a balloon at the rim, and dripped onto the table. A fleck of the froth fell onto the wing of the Cabbage White, leaving a puce smudge.

Soon the cream spots on the fore-wings of the Crimson Tiger were coloured puce. Gerald took a bent pin mounted on a pencil stump, and with it gently extended the left fore-wing, revealing the crimson underwing. The tiger was wonderful to see, gayer by far than hitherto, a Rainbow Tiger, a Joseph in his coat of many colours. But he slept on unmoved, quite ignorant of the wonderful changes that had overtaken him.

His work done, Gerald put the supine Moth in the box and clapped on the glass lid. He did not kill the Moth lest he should turn out to be a Crimson Tigress after all, and deposit a batch of eggs on the bottom of the box — eggs which would presently hatch out into a host of squirming caterpillars, that he would rear in a cage till they became fat and full grown. Then they would turn into chrysalids, remain dormant all the winter, and emerge as a bevy of Crimson Tigers in the following June.

Would the children inherit the rainbow hues of the parent? Gerald was in doubt as to this. But the more he thought about it, the more pleased he became with the idea, the more certain he felt that the brood would resemble its distinguished mother. What an achievement! How skilfully, at the cost of what pains of thought and expenditure of chemicals, with what magnificent outcome, had Art been wedded to Nature! How great the stir when some luckless member of the race of Puce Tigers is captured by an eager hunter, sold for a fabulous sum of money, figured in the journals of Natural History Societies! What a thing to have done, to have invented the Hopperley Puce Tiger and made Natural History!

Gerald took the Puce Tiger upstairs with him that night, putting his (or her) box on the table beside the bed. Early in the morning he searched the bottom and sides of the box, and even ruffled the Tiger's fur to see if an egg had been mislaid, but nowhere could he find a trace of one. It was very disappointing. He searched again in the afternoon, without success. The Puce Tiger was probably a male.

Gerald's brain devised another scheme, one bristling with risks, a poor substitute for the one that had failed, but one that might, given luck, serve to perpetuate the race of Puce Tigers. If the Tiger were released he would doubtless come upon a Crimson Tigress, and become a Father. Some of his offspring should take after him. But there remained a risk, an awful possibility that the Tiger would fail to meet the Tigress, that he or she would suffer a premature death, that disaster would overtake the young brood. On the other hand, Gerald recalled the injunction to cast one's bread upon the waters with the assurance that after many days it will return.

He decided to give the whole matter his consideration.

III

It had been arranged that Gerald should call upon Mr Tetrapod that evening and proceed with that gentleman to a street not far distant, there to catch the moths that hovered round a brilliant arc lamp. Gerald collected his apparatus — his net of fine green gauze, his bamboo rods that fitted into one another so that the net should reach to a great height, his cyanide bottle and collecting boxes. Armed with these, carrying also the Puce Tiger in his pocket, he set out for Mr Tetrapod's.

Gerald found Tetrapod in the murky hole that he euphemistically termed his study. Actually it was his bedroom, dining room, drawing room and moth box rolled into one and overlaid with a blanket of dust. A plate of nibbled breakfast sausage and a killing-bottle lay on the unmade bed; a solitary bed sock (it was high June, mind you) rested in the middle of the floor; in the bottom of the wash bowl there were a pair of spectacles and an empty sardine tin. All round the room, stacked from floor to ceiling, were boxes of butterflies, moths and beetles, gathered from the four corners of the earth. But Mr Tetrapod came near to being the strangest specimen of them all. Some said that he resembled the scorpion that always hung in a glass case over the fireplace. Gerald thought that he was like Mrs Spool, the Hopperleys' charwoman, so awry and birdy was his countenance, so crooked and bony his body. Tetrapod was mad, of course, but Gerald did not notice that. The only characteristic of Tetrapod's which Gerald whole-heartedly deplored was his air of omniscience, his overweening scorn for Gerald's most elaborate theories, the derision with which he regarded Gerald's choicest specimens.

Gerald, having netted a rare and curious moth, would take it along to Tetrapod, sticking out his chest with collector's pride.

"Yes yes yes my boy," old Tetrapod would croak, "Very good, very good. A Canary-shouldered Thorn, Ennomos alniaria, female, quite common in marshy places and woods. Caught three at a time the other day. Rubbish. Threw them away. Rubbish."

Or, "Yes of course, a Wormwood Pug, Eupithecia absinthiata, common as flies in a place I know. Still I must congratulate you on the way you've set it, though it's as common as… as…" he would look about the room, hunting for a word, "it's as common as muck."

Then he would fetch down a case, open it, raising a dust-storm, and show Gerald a battalion of Wormwood Pugs pinned to the cork lid. Gerald would depart with sorrow in his heart, vowing to catch a moth that would startle even the redoubtable Tetrapod.

So far, Gerald had failed to extract one syllable of applause from Tetrapod. But today he had a surprise, O what a surprise, for the old fellow!

Boldly he walked up to the table, fingering the box in his pocket.

Between Tetrapod's spectacles (he was wearing two pairs) and the book he was reading, there suddenly appeared the Tiger, black, viridian, crimson and puce. For the space of about a second his eyes rested quite calmly upon the Moth. Then, as they appreciated to the full the phenomenon that confronted them, they grew wild, they darted forth, a bright light shone in them. Tetrapod sprang from his seat and stood swaying with the box clutched in his hand.

The miraculous effect of the Puce Tiger startled even Gerald, its Author. A just pride welled in his bosom.

Tetrapod, still swaying, was peering closely at the Moth through his double spectacles, and gasping:

"Lord a mercy... Lord a mercy..."

Gerald interrupted: "I caught him."

"Where, where?" cried Tetrapod.

"By the arc lamp."

"My boy, my boy," Tetrapod grasped Gerald's hand. His voice shook with emotion. "Do you know that this Moth is practically unthinkable, the biggest freak since I caught... since..."

"Yes," said Gerald, immodestly.

Tetrapod laid the Tiger on the table and looked at Gerald with eyes so horribly magnified by the double glasses that they looked like a pair of damsons.

"It's all right, is it?" he said anxiously. "No monkey tricks, no funny business this time, hey?" He recalled the time when Gerald had deceived him with a white mouse (Gerald had made the mouse drink a queer brew that had turned its ears and nostrils a kind of heliotrope), and certain other quite unscrupulous tricks that Gerald had played upon him.

Gerald said in an injured voice, "Oh Mr Tetrapod, how could

you suggest such a thing?"

Tetrapod shook his head. The youthful Gerald, his most ardent disciple, close friend and unrelenting tormentor, was a boy of parts, but some of the parts troubled Tetrapod.

He took up the Tiger again.

"There's something odd about those flea-coloured spots, something mighty queer. Wait here." he said to Gerald, "while I get my microscope. I left it in the larder."

He ran out of the room, leaving Gerald standing by the table.

Quickly Gerald's mind worked. What if Tetrapod, aided by the microscope, should discover the origin of the puce and viridian spots? Would their friendship stand the strain of another deception laid bare? Assuredly it would not. Then the Tiger must go. It would break his heart, but the Puce Tiger must be set free, this instant, before Tetrapod came back. And perhaps the Tiger would meet the Tigress…

Tetrapod's footfall sounded in the passage outside.

In a moment Gerald had whipped up the box, taken off its lid, run with it to the window, which by some lucky chance was open a couple of inches, and shaken the box violently. He darted back with the empty box and put it on the table, precisely at the moment when Tetrapod put his hand on the door-nob.

A veil must be drawn over the greater part of the scene that followed. The expressions which Tetrapod used were not fit for Gerald's youthful ears; certainly it would be improper in me to write them down.

Gerald, of course, protested that the Moth was his; that he, as its proprietor, had an inalienable right to lift the lid; that the Moth, being a moth, had desired to fly and had accordingly made straight-way for the window—a very sensible thing to do; and that when all's said and done, Mr Tetrapod shouldn't leave his window open.

To all these arguments Tetrapod furnished no printable reply.

Throughout their journey to the arc lamp, Gerald and he were not on speaking terms. Gerald was thinking tenderly and anxiously about the Puce Tiger, of the Tiger's love affairs, of the dangers that beset him, of the family he might raise.

Tetrapod was on the horns of a dilemma. Should he write to the Entomological Press concerning this marvellous Tiger and compose a monograph about it, or should he regard the Moth as a monster, a creation of young Hopperley's fiendishly ingenious brain?

Neither of them noticed, sailing high in the air over their heads, the Puce Tiger.

IV

The Puce Tiger tumbled over and over. Down, down, he fell, still sleeping, till his headlong motion aroused him with a start, just as he was about to hit the ground. In the nick of time he stretched his wings, buffeted the air and floated away.

The night air was cool, deliciously refreshing after his long slumber. It tasted like wine, pungent, exhilarating. It buoyed him, lifting his crimson body with ethereal fingers. It ruffled and soothed the fur of his back with kisses, singing little songs to him with the rustle of his wings.

Over the Town the Tiger sailed, towards the North. Without so much as a glance for his relative, he swept past the Weather-vane. For a moment he stayed his flight by the cross-gartered moon. Had he listened intently he would have heard a little voice, proceeding from under the moon:

"Mr Tetrapod, Mr Tetrapod. Supposing, just supposing, a white mouse was to topple into an ink-pot, would she have blue children?"

And he would have heard a blood-curdling yell, a scream, a crashing of glass, a scuffling as of a Man and a Boy fighting.

But the Puce Tiger did not hear. He did not see the shattering of the cross-gartered moon. Other, more entrancing, visions filled his mind. Swooping down towards the earth, he saw a Tigress, resplendent under the stars, a matchless Moth that stirred his soul to the depths.

She was the loveliest sight he had ever set eyes on. Starlight glazed her crimson back, her vermeil wing, her viridian eye-markings. His thoughts became a Poem, his desire a Furnace.

He plunged.

But her touch was cold, ice-cold; her beauty an airy thing that vanished; her love the embrace of Death itself.

He had drowned himself in a horse-trough.

In the morning they found him, a Crimson Tiger once more, with his viridian and puce spots all but washed away, floating on the surface of the water.

Such was the passing of the Puce Tiger, the first and last of his line, the Melchisedec among Tigers.

* * *

Chapter 14

The Nightmare Nose

As I lay in bed I heard them whisper that I was mad. But I am not mad. In the night when they thought I was asleep, one of them said, "He had a fit, poor boy," and the other replied, "He will die."

They know nothing about me, and I shall keep my secret until I die, in a week perhaps or a month from now. Then they will read this and know that I was not mad. I do not want their pity. I want them to understand, and if they understand they will not call me mad.

Mad indeed!

Today I am nineteen years old, but it began when I was a child, about nine years ago. I was playing in my uncle's garden with my cousin Jacqueline. We had stretched a linen line across the lawn and were playing "tennis". Quite suddenly she stopped and, looking at my face, cried,

"Oh, you've a red nose!"

Then she laughed and ran into the house.

That was how it began. Perhaps you will laugh at what I write and will say, "Began? What began, you fool? So this is the great event!" Trivial enough it seems to you, no doubt. But those words of Jacqueline's turned my life.

I followed her indoors and went up to the bathroom. She was right. There it was in the mirror, long, with a kind of swelling at the end of it. The upper part was pale like my cheeks, but the bump at the end was red. Somehow it reminded me of a strawberry, or the dome of a minaret. It had a horrid, an obscene significance. Then I went to my bedroom and looked in the mirror of the wardrobe. But here the window was very low and the light cast shadows upwards, so that the redness was almost invisible. But in my aunt's room it was red again, redder than ever. I looked at it from every angle, using the swinging side-mirrors of her dressing table. The side view was almost normal. It was the front view that looked so terrible.

That night I lay in bed and knew that I would have to live my life through with this thing, uncovered and shameful, in the midst of my face. Not so much its ugliness — though indeed it was ugly — but its shamefulness appalled me. It was there as a portent and evidence of evil. In some obscure way it stood as a symbol of vileness before God and man. Just before I had gone to stay with my uncle, my father had warned me about some matters concerning my body. So far from heeding his warnings, I had experimented, had gone on experimenting... Perhaps God was punishing me in this way.

When I returned home from my uncle's house I began to notice how people looked at me. The boys at school sometimes laughed outright and older folk stared queerly. One day, when I had been told to stand in front of the class, the master changed his mind and said,

"No, you can go back, you're not an ornament."

I knew what he meant. He had one of the whitest, smallest, shapeliest noses I have ever seen.

Often during the first year or two I was able to forget. Sometimes for a whole hour, when reading or playing, I would not think once of my disfigurement. On rare occasions during the holidays, when I was entirely absorbed in drawing and painting, I would spend almost a whole day in blessed oblivion.

Such moments of respite became fewer as I grew older. Whether it was that my eyes had sunk a little or that I had not noticed it before, but I was able to see the tip of my nose when looking downwards, and so the horrid reminder was always before me, never allowing me any peace of mind. I used to shrink from the daylight. I would never walk home from school by the main street and along the crowded pavements, for everyone there stared at me with pitiful derision. Whenever it was possible I used to walk by the almost deserted side streets and alleys, and always tried to get to school just before the bell rang, so that I should be with the boys as little as possible.

In the tramcar, by which I travelled when it was raining, on Sunday at church, at night from my window overlooking the street, I used to watch the faces of the people. Their noses were pale and beautiful. Lovely men and women, boys and girls! Happy, not alone and abominable to men, God had not cursed them. Stinking old women, full of dirt-creased wrinkles, with beards sprouting from their shrivelled chins, dragging themselves along the pavement, seemed to me blessed. They suffered for ugliness but not for shame. Their condition was proper to their age and circumstances, acceptable to men and not a thing to be derided. Most gladly would I have changed bodies with the foulest of them. There lived in our town a woman with lupus, whom I had often seen with a shawl over most of her face, leaving only one ghastly red-rimmed eye exposed. One day I saw her standing at her door talking to a neighbour. In the middle of her scarred and eaten face there was a raw patch with two black holes. Here at last was my equal, my sister, a creature like myself.

Nevertheless each season brought with it some measure of relief, or I think I should have died. In the summer I used to lie in the sun, till my face was burnt red and then brown. How well I remember the summer of my thirteenth year, returning home after a day in the very hot sunshine, and my face in the mirror with ruddy cheeks and glowing forehead! I looked healthy and normal. I was brimming over with joy. Immediately people were kind to me; they loved me and I loved them. I could look into their faces and laugh, without confusion. Yes, I laughed!

Soon my cheeks paled again and I laughed no longer. It became my dearest wish to live in some southern land where the hot sun always shines. There I could be happy. But the long winter evenings brought respite. Then I could walk with the people in the street and hold up my head among them. In the half darkness I would almost pass for one of them. And in the house the lamplight was kind to me.

I could never accept with humility my affliction, but was constantly occupied in devising means for its alleviation. The first expedient that occurred to me was to paint my nose. I bought for this purpose a tube of Chinese white colour and daubed it on with my finger. It looked too obvious, so I mixed a kind of pink, but this again appeared quite unnatural. During these experiments I happened to notice a tube of toothpaste lying on the bathroom shelf. This proved to be far more effective. When the light shone downwards and was strong, my nose was still red, but of a lighter shade, and indoors it looked nearly normal.

A red nose has qualities of its own. It is quite unlike red eyes, red ears or pimples, unlike the scars and stigmata of sickness. Not one of these is funny or really shameful. But a red nose is a joke, obscene and piteous. It has—I cannot say how or what—a meaning, a disgraceful ridiculousness that all other disfigurements lack. All those people—I suppose some four or five of them—who have made some remark about my nose in my presence, whether to myself or to others, have laughed, and laughed almost as though the joke were indecent. I have never heard anyone laugh at the most hideous scar on the face, at a suppurating wound in any part of the body, at a legless or armless man or at a corpse. There are no jokes about leprosy. Why did they laugh at me?

The whole process is so shameful to me that I can only write of it because I am going to die. I have never spoken to anyone of it. All the while I think of it I am more ashamed than I would be of any crime that man has committed, of mutilation or rape or murder. For other things people would hate or fear me. For this I am a despicable thing, a worm. To be a romantic villain or terrible monster would be endurable. The triviality of my curse is part of its horror.

But now I do not care. I will conceal nothing, but heap shame upon shame. Yes, I have daubed toothpaste on my nose for eight year. That, in a sentence, is the true story of my youth. Glorious childhood, Life's morning, the Springtime of all our years—is that how men speak of youth? For me it has been—toothpaste smeared on the end of a nose that was shaped somewhat like a strawberry!

For eight years I have carried about in my pocket a little tin containing a lump of toothpaste and a piece of mirror, and every morning, midday and evening I have seen the gloss and redness of my nose and smeared it with paste. There arose several difficulties. The paste, for instance, was washed away by rain. Whenever it rained I tried by every means to avoid going out of doors. If that were impossible I would pull my cap down over my eyes. If the rain still blew into my face the only course left was to rub off the paste with my handkerchief. Then, if anyone were approaching I would cross the road or pretend to blow my nose till I was alone again.

Sometimes it was possible to see the paste, when the light was strong or after I had been sweating. One day at school, when I was sixteen, a boy looked at me and shouted,

"Look, he's powdered his nose!"

The boys crowded round and came close to my face. One of them touched my nose with his finger and brought off a smudge of white, and the other boys did the same. Then they let me go and I ran into the lavatories, where I writhed in violent sickness till I fell down and lay in the dirt. For a week after I lay in bed pretending, long after I had recovered, to be ill, lest my parents should make me go back to school.

The fact that in many ways I despised those boys was no solace to me. In every intellectual pursuit and in the appreciation of beauty I was certain of my superiority. But such things were not honourable among them. In their eyes, and in my own, a comely face was of far more account than any spiritual excellence. An idiot with a little white nose was a god, and I was a creeping thing.

I cannot tell you of my feelings during the ten years of my affliction. How can I convey to you, who are normal and unafflicted, what life has held for me? You can know nothing of these depths of shame. Can you imagine them, or will you laugh too?

I never thought seriously of taking my life. I think my agony was too great for that. I never wholly despaired, for despair is near to resignation and resignation is not far from content. Always, lurking in the back of my mind, there was hope. This hope was founded upon several possibilities. I had heard of the marvels of plastic surgery, of faces dreadfully mutilated during the war, of cheeks and noses blown away, that had been wonderfully restored by the grafting of flesh. Why, I thought, should this not be done for me? But I could speak of it to no one.

Then one day I found in the columns of a magazine a small announcement:

"RED NOSES

ABSOLUTELY CURED

Write for free booklet to..."

Excitedly I tore out the advertisement. My parents would of course demand to know the contents of any letter that I received, so I begged them to let me go away, saying that I needed a change. For months I had to wait, till at last it was arranged that I should stay at my uncle's again. As soon as I arrived I posted a letter to the advertiser and received in reply a pamphlet containing a list of testimonials from people that had been cured by the — system, and announcing that the price of the treatment was two guineas. Here was another obstacle, for I had little more than two shillings. After much difficulty I managed to persuade a pawnbroker to give me two pounds for my watch, fountain pen and overcoat. The man appeared to be convinced that I had stolen them. Perhaps when my parents read this they will forgive me for the fantastic story which I invented to explain the loss of my property.

The parcel arrived by registered post. For days my elation had been steadily increasing. I loved to picture myself, in a fortnight or a month's time, as normal, and to make the boldest plans. I knew that my affliction was the only thing that stood between me and all that I desired. I was absolutely certain that, if I were cured, I could then do anything that I set my heart upon. Without limit I would excel, and compel the admiration of my despisers.

Trembling with hope I opened the packet. It contained a green bottle labelled "The Lotion"—a pinkish sediment in what appeared to be water, a box holding six large red-coated pills and twelve smaller brown ones, and a few sheets of type-written instructions. The gist of the latter was that a red nose is, as a rule, a symptom of indigestion and general ill-health, and that it was necessary to regulate one's diet, masticate thoroughly, and take plenty of exercise. The pills were to be taken at specified intervals and the lotion applied before going to bed.

So far as I was able I followed these instruction. It was, of course, impossible to change my food to the prescribed diet, but, by pretending to be ill and to dislike certain foods, I had a wider choice. All the rest I obeyed to the letter, till the pills were all taken and the bottle was empty. Dozens of times I went to look in my mirror, and surveyed my face anxiously from every angle. Sometimes there seemed to be an improvement and I would do bold things — walk down the main street in broad daylight, look people in the face, arrive early at school and talk to the boys. At other times there appeared to be no change, or even a change for the worse. Then I would lie on my bed, bury my face in the pillow, and pray for an accident that would crush my face, tear the flesh, mutilate it horribly. At that time lupus, even leprosy, seemed desirable.

My enemies, those who laughed at my face and wondered at my crestfallenness and fear of people, will not despise me the less for these confessions. But wait, your judgment may be premature! I too, even I, the child who feared the street, the boy with the toothpaste and the mirror, the youth with the loathsome blister for a nose — even I have had my moments. And possibly — I do not know — those moments have been such as you have never known. Perhaps, after all, God has some kindness for those whom he curses.

A few occasions stand out as vivid splashes of colour across the forlorn grey pattern of my life. Especially I remember one frosty evening long ago, when the world had been transformed by a thin covering of snow and the stinging air was absolutely still. Over the fields we raced playing football till the whole sky sparkled with stars, and after that we fought with snowballs, shouting and laughing as we hit one another and threw up shining fountains of snow. A rushing thrill of triumph, a torrent of wild joy, possessed me. Gloriously I ran and ran, beautiful in a beautiful world. Ah, that dazzling night!

Of such a kind were the visions which shone like jewels in the sombre setting of my nightmare life. But I had another, a real life. You who knew me as a shrinking pallid youth, who thought me stupid as well as ugly—how little you knew me! You knew less of my inmost self than of the remotest stranger's. You were dream people. You, and I among you, were chimaeras conjured up from some foul nether world. You affirm your reality. I deny it. You say that I am mad. But you and all you say are the figment of a dream. I say that you do not exist. I abjure you. When my true self possesses me I laugh. I sneer at the self of my dreams, at this poor creature that dares to call itself by my name, and I deride and disown all who know me thus. With angry impatience I mock at you, inventions of an evil imagination. The essence of life, the true self—how can these have part in such a condition?

A red nose, daubed with toothpaste!

Such unheroic misery, such ludicrous trifles, are they of the stuff of life? Is the world like this? You claim reality, and my doom is that for half of my life I believe you, and am persuaded that the beauty is unsubstantial.

But if you must be real, at least I will claim that my own world has reality too. I will tell you of this world that I enjoyed, though I shall never convey the true quality of its beauty to you. I do not care if you deride. It is beyond your reach.

I saw the world as an emerald flood, flowing endlessly, strewn with myrtle trees and tightly clustered woodlands. Over all, poised in a saucer sky, climbed frothing cloud masses, seething and bubbling at their rims. Like giant snowmen they tumbled clumsily, in an orgy of plunging and rearing, from horizon to horizon, and among them floated an aerial being, a god. The dolorous bird's cry in the woods at sundown did not escape his ear. Tiny flowers like fragments of the moon, amid the grass, ashen wisps of wood-smoke swirling upwards, dew-sparkling leaves and boughs laden with fruit trembling in sunny gales, butterflies whose wings outshone the deep turquoise pools of water—in all these he took pleasure. The first crocus flamed above the snow for him alone. At sunset, cloud billows drenched with blood-red light played beneath him and his hair floated in apple-green whorls of sky. When all heaven writhed in a fury of thunder crashes and forked lightnings he was there, roaring and shouting and singing in the caverns between the clouds.

He was — oh, noble! From the blackness of the night sifted stars shone down on a profile so blue-pale, so more than Greek in its suave splendour! In the daytime the earth's animation and his own overflux merged in a common radiance. The vigour of all things that grow, the souls of all plants and animals, all brooding terrestrial spirits, entered his spirit, so that he held aloof from none of the forms of life. And always he swept along with the feeling of triumph, of participation in all striving and conquest, of the ecstasy of power exercising itself in the limitless spaces that lie above the earth.

Such a being I worshipped. And in some mysterious way he was myself. When I thought of him, as often I did, I was at once an onlooker and the being himself. Through his eyes I saw all the world spread out below me; every sensation of speed and might and joy I shared with him. Especially his features were mine. I revelled in the knowledge of their possession, yet I could look upon them. His body I knew; it melted, as it were, into a cloud.

No men and women lived in our world. Great malevolent spirits and cloud-shapes there were, evil and glowering over against us. But we always prevailed over them, overcoming them with a set purpose. Nothing that we did was without this sense of victory, of purpose about to be accomplished. I know what this purpose was, but no words can compass it.

And this, you would say, is a dream world, a madman's paradise, a lie! You would have me embrace what you call the truth! Hell, they say, is terrible torment, but it seems to me that Hell is supreme torture only to those who have come from Heaven. If I had never found my own world, then doubtless I should have borne more easily the gnawing pain of yours. Daily I came down from a place of wonderful loveliness, not to some grand Hell of heroic suffering, but to a banal torment. Glorious tragedies are not written around red noses and toothpaste. With the memory of indescribable delights fresh in my mind, I shudder at those words, the horror of ten years.

But the nightmare is over. Jacqueline who began it ended it. She grew up a tall, flaxen haired girl, and more and more I loved her. A week ago she came to stay at my home, and we went walking the fields. After a time we rested. Sitting with my back to her, I said:

"Jacqueline, I adore you."

She laughed, "Not really?"

"Yes really."

Then we were silent.

All the while I cursed my folly. That she should walk with me where there was no one to see was wonderful enough; to be seen with me was more than such a girl could endure; but to love me — why, that was unthinkable madness. What devilish prompting it was that made me speak so to her, I do not know.

At last I said, "Why don't you like me? Is it..." but I could not say it.

I turned to her, forgetting the tears that were rolling down my face. She was smiling.

I left her and ran home. In my bedroom mirror I saw it, streaked with the tears. She had seen...

Then I found a razor and went back to the mirror.

I remember no pain, only a gush of blood and the dripping flesh hanging down over my upper lip. The razor touched the bone and would go no further, so I jabbed at the other side, and the blood rose in my nostrils and flowed down my throat. A dripping mass fell onto the dressing table.

Then a strange desire came over me. I half covered my face with a scarf and rushed out of doors. Along the street I ran, while the hot blood trickled down my neck and chest, till I stood before the cottage of the woman with lupus. The door was ajar, and I went in.

In her little sordid room she stood, with her arms folded, gaping at me. Her face was one large sore and her eyes stared at me in their bloody rims. Ripping the scarf from my head I advanced towards her, stretching out my arms.

"I am... I..." But the blood came too fast. I fell. The last thing I remember was the taste of the blood.

I awoke in this place, and here I shall presently die. Then they will find this.

Will they think I was mad?

* * *

CPSIA information can be obtained
at www.ICGtesting.com
Printed in the USA
FSHW010605101218
54360FS